CHRIST ON THE RUE JACOB

BOOKS BY SEVERO SARDUY
AVAILABLE IN ENGLISH TRANSLATION

FICTION
From Cuba with a Song
Cobra
Maitreya

LITERARY ESSAYS
Written on a Body

RADIO PLAYS
For Voice

CHRIST ON THE RUE JACOB

SEVERO SARDUY

TRANSLATED BY
SUZANNE JILL LEVINE AND
CAROL MAIER

MERCURY HOUSE  SAN FRANCISCO

© 1987 Severo Sarduy and the heirs of Severo Sarduy. Originally published in Spanish by Edicions del Mall as *El Cristo de la rue Jacob*. English translation © 1995 by Suzanne Jill Levine and Carol Maier

Excerpt from *The Lover* by Marguerite Duras, translated Barbara Bray. Translation © 1985 by Random House, Inc. and William Collins Sons & Company, Ltd. Reprinted by permission of Pantheon Books, a division of Random House, Inc.

Published in the United States by Mercury House, San Francisco, California, a nonprofit publishing company devoted to the free exchange of ideas and guided by a dedication to literary values.

United States Constitution, First Amendment: Congress shall make no law respecting an establishment of religion, or prohibiting the free exercise thereof; or abridging the freedom of speech, or of the press; or the right of the people peaceably to assemble, and to petition the Government for a redress of grievances.

Mercury House and colophon are registered trademarks of Mercury House, Incorporated. Printed on recycled acid-free paper. Manufactured in the United States of America. Text design by David Peattie using Sabon.

Library of Congress Cataloging-in-Publication Data

Sarduy, Severo.
   [El Cristo de la rue Jacob. English]
   Christ on the Rue Jacob / by Severo Sarduy ; translated by Suzanne Jill Levine and Carol Maier
     p.   cm. ISBN 1-56279-075-7 (pbk.)
   I. Levine, Suzanne Jill. II. Maier, Carol. III. Title.
PQ7390.S28C713   1995
864—DC20   94-37259
                                 CIP

FIRST EDITION
5   4   3   2   1

Contents

Preface   vii

I. ARCHAEOLOGY OF THE SKIN

A Thorn in My Skull   4
Four Stitches in My Right Eyebrow   8
Scar   17
Two Broken Uppers, a Stitch in My
    Lower Lip, or Christ on the Rue Jacob 23
Omphalos   28
A Wart on My Foot   32

II. LESSONS IN THE EPHEMERAL

UNITY OF PLACE
Benares   38
Wearing Space   48
Tangier   51

BECAUSE IT'S REAL
The Stratagem of the Tick   56
Café de Flore   58
A Cleaning   68

UNITY OF FIGURE
The Jungle   72
The House of Raquel Vega   74
Heaven and Earth   77
Severo, Why Do You Paint?   84

BECAUSE IT'S REAL

An Image of Christ's Ascent   90
Texts for Nothing   93
Soldiers   95
The Street Cleaner of Mexico City   97

ON AN AUTUMN NIGHT,
  I THINK OF MY FRIENDS

The Tibetan Book of the Dead   101
Portraits by Jesse   107
At Eight in the Flore   112
Dream   119
Last Postcard to Emir   124
Letter from Lezama   128

Translators' Afterword   156

EFACEPREFACEPREFACEPREFACEPREFACEPR
FACEPREFACEPREFACEPREFACEPREFACEPR
FACEPREFACEPREFACEPREFACEPREFACEPR
FACEPREFACEPREFACEPREFACEPREFACEPR
FACEPREFACEPREFACEPREFACEPREFACEPR
FACEPREFACEPREFACEPREFACEPREFACEPR
ACEPREFACEPREFACEPREFACEPREFACEPR
ACEPREFACEPREFACEPREFACEPREFACEPR

PREFACE

I have gathered in this volume what for a long time I called "epiphanies": in an age starved for religion, everything gets baptized a name that might couple it with the absolute.

The pieces, however, are really about imprints, marks, above all physical marks—what remains written on the body. By surveying these scars from my head down to my feet, I have sketched a possible autobiography, summarized in an archaeology of the skin. The only thing that matters in one's personal story is whatever has been ciphered on the body and thus continues to talk, to narrate, to simulate the incident responsible for its inscription.

The whole forms a narrative maquette, a model: by reading the body's scars, anyone could write a personal archaeology, describe the body's tattoos in a different blue ink.

The second part is also an inventory of marks, not physical but mnemonic: what remains in memory, more indelible than a recollection but less intense than an obsession. Images — of a city, of a painting — incidents, events, deaths. A chance encounter in the woods, after the flight of a deer; a banal but unforgettable phrase; the photograph of a little girl trapped amid debris, who will die seconds later and is bidding farewell to her loved ones; a letter from Lezama Lima; a few paragraphs to complete the posthumous text of a friend.

These are neither articles nor essays, nor commentaries on images or painting: their genre is ambiguous, their definition precise. They are neither the vain manipulation of knowledge nor showy textuality. They are traces left by things ephemeral, always surviving their frayage* or their substance. They constitute a record of things that — sometimes by chance — once put me in touch with something. Epiphanies after all.

*François Wahl explains that the term "comes from Freud, to designate the passage (or non-passage) of stimuli in the nerve synaspses. S. alludes to the passage of the event, its occurrence and disappearance." (Letter to SJL, March 17, 1995)

CHRIST ON THE RUE JACOB

I
ARCHAEOLOGY OF THE SKIN

A Thorn in My Skull

At that time we were very close, my mother and I; we were literally almost the same person. She would hold me tight so that I would fall asleep; I would slide my feet between the couch and her thighs, in order to feel the weight of her body.

In one of those jousts of eloquence imposed by slow trains, she admitted to me that sometimes she would go without eating so I could have more. What I told her was something the blacks talked about: how they had seen the lame whore, the one wooed by the stationmaster — my father — walk between two cars of a train. She wore silver-rimmed glasses and a dark scaly dress that shone with a soft greenish glow as she walked.

—

Jumping on a trapdoor over the cellar filled with machinery, my sister had fallen in; my father was pulling the huge nickel-plated levers to let the train through. We leapt down there frantically in order to rescue her.

—

I had gone fishing for *guajacones*. I used to wait entire afternoons in the stillness of the pond until they swam into a perfume bottle I then covered with my hand. As I ran, I passed under the orange tree. I felt nothing when the thorn embedded itself into my skull.

—

The surgeon made a slit with his tiny scalpel. A strong smell of ether, a dense, opaque red in the jar of Mercurochrome. A soft tinkling: polished surgical instruments going by on a small cart. The island humidity misted the white tiles on the walls.

The icy feel of the anesthetic as it touched my head plunged me into myself. The pain was mine.

This was not my mother's body that suffered, that fought stubbornly against the wound, that was reflected distortedly and asymmetrically by the sweaty tiles and handled by the officiating priest. This matter was different, a different expanse, its boundaries had been burned in blood, its edges blazed.

In the interstice of that minute wound, we separated in pain. I knew now that I was the owner of a different skin, of different ganglia, a mute medley of muscles that awakened a different thirst. I understood then that this "bunch of nerves" — as I was christened by the nurse who fortified me with intravenous feedings in the kitchen of a huge colonial house — could also be awakened by a different handling, a different touch that I barely suspected, one sensitive to the shadows of the other side, to the opposing sphere of the thorn, to pleasure's camera obscura.

Four Stitches
in My Right Eyebrow

Finally I understood: I was struggling, as I began this "epiphany," which is what I persist in calling these fragile vignettes that illustrate the reading of my body — as if it were possible to glimpse in them the flash of a revelation — struggling with the same impossibility that prevented me from continuing my novel about Colibrí the hummingbird, when the incident of the *mark* occurred.

Every writer, from the time his bent becomes apparent, with the first faint signs of talent, suspects that it falls to his lot to live a lesser apocalypse preceding the days that will end the world. Every writer suspects that the pages so laboriously put together — with whatever manages to escape the erasures and drafts that always end up restoring one's original word — constitute the last book his energy, or the distilled metaphor of narcissism we call inspiration, will grant him.

Such was the conundrum I found myself confronting as I began *Colibrí* with neither a good grasp of the characters nor the writing that would flesh them out, and without a hint of a plot. I was filled with anxiety: interrupting that long sentence we begin as we are born — to writing — is like approaching the death of speech. The characters faced each other in simulated combat, in a struggle prolonged by the novel to the point of boredom. Colibrí's fierce, treacherous, enormous Japanese enemy crashed into a mannered mural of a winter landscape. What was going to happen next?

I set him on his feet, eyes lowered — no doubt he'd been humiliated by the unsuccessful skirmish — and then all I could manage was a string of three adjectives: "Intact. Statuesque. Unscathed." After that line, nothing. Round and round in circles. Dejection. Self-critical masochism and the total lack of confidence that nothing can repair except, around noon, repeated glasses of beer.

—

Like a screen at once translucent and dense, alcoholic persistence and its deceptive security form a soft filter between the eyes of the thirsty writer and rough reality.

You resort to this intoxication, I told myself, because you feel that God denies you true intoxication, true euphoria: beholding something, even something trivial, you have created yourself; inventing a place as real as the one in which you write, or a character made of words and their intricate weave, but a credible character nevertheless; finding an adjective, surprising, nonfunctional, even eccentric, yet splendidly precise and relevant all the same, as if it provides the attribute the noun requested from the beginning, requested silently, and which now, cleaning and polishing the metal of your worn-out language, you came upon unexpectedly, as if it had been whispered to you by a generous demiurge. Another beer.

The prose of *beeromania* has yet to be written. I'm not speaking, of course, about the self-absorbed, chronic alcoholism already studied in the vast, complementary literatures of Repression and Medicine, but about the benign albeit compulsive celebration that aspires only to the state of "happiness," to momentary irresponsibility, to a letting go, around the brief noon hour, of the weight of one's self, of the punctual watchfulness of the Other in the omnipresent shape of the Law.

Like a death mask, perfectly round — an ashen moon, an old coin, a sucking mouth or excreting anus — the O of the Other pops up everywhere, behind people and things, as if its little smile were the only bond connecting them, the only access they had to irrevocable authority.

Alcoholism stupefies the thirsty subject and deprives him of the day's fundamental continuity, transporting him to an inane, mechanical, dreamlike limbo with its aftermath of teariness, tiresome repetitions, and discordant guffaws. Beeromania both hypertrophies and dulls. It shuffles time: what happened before, what happened after? What violent calm or insulting intensity accompanied the events? Where did they really take place? With whom? Dawn, wiping the slate clean but leaving a very rough first draft in the scribbles not quite erased, arrives with neither vomiting nor hangover, tinged only with a disquieting familiarity.

—

With overbrimmings both foamy and uric, in the last analysis beeromania does not just emanate like the sweat that forms on a cold glass; it emanates from anxiety, from the feeling that one has been totally abandoned.

Someone with whom we were physically united — we were almost the same person — reveals to us, with a single sentence, the *extent* to which we have been abandoned, as if drawing back a curtain to show us an excessive landscape.

The gesture with which we are abandoned is so unexpected and theatrical that this person inevitably comes to occupy the place of God.

We are helpless against such a withdrawal. Like faith, presence is a gift; it is a contribution that one cannot prompt, a gratuity, almost a whim.

We cannot interrogate — barely formulated here, this question constitutes Elie Wiesel's entire work — one who is absent about this detachment, since it derives from an individual's free will; we can only ask ingenuously, almost grotesquely, where he was when the disaster of our abandonment occurred.

All we can do, then, is shuffle time, return, repeatedly but only for an instant, in the flashes of mirages and moments, to an illusory before: before time turned into an enemy, in the mythical era of identity and protection. The fourth beer provides that breath of compassionate complicity.

—

No one believes, ever, that I'm sick, that stage fright has me terrorized, or that the alcohol sweeps me along in its imperceptible surge — no one except my mother — thanks to the rhythm of my respiration. So great is my purely animal capacity for defensive camouflage and simulation.

I feigned, then — as I discovered the next day — enough lucidity in the shuffled time of that afternoon to monopolize the proliferating table talk, and later the less involved, almost utilitarian conversation that negotiated both my encounter with D. and his subsequent return, with me at the wheel, to the neighboring village.

A series of obscure, discontinuous images. I fall headlong against the sink, a bilious vomit floods the basin, I look at myself in the mirror — a stream of dark, almost coagulated blood spurts from my right eyebrow, which was cut by the faucet. I stanch the bleeding by pressing a towel against my forehead and eye; perhaps I fall asleep. I run to the caretaker's house; I simulate once again and drive to the hospital.

With the same hateful talent people have for table talk, I amuse the doctors throughout the operation.

—

I did not know for certain what had happened. I conjured up multiple and contradictory versions. In the most persistent, a naked D. attacked me with an obsidian knife. You could hear strange birds that were not local but from a calm, transparent lake surrounded by prickly pear trees. In the distance there was also the sound of tambourines and maracas. Another version involved a ritual of self-mutilation offered under drugs to an unknown god. In another, I slipped in my garden at home, running with some yellow dogs that bristled with spines. The trees cast black and blue shadows.

I did not know for certain what had happened.

What I did know was how the chapter of *Colibrí* continued: "Intact. Statuesque. Unscathed. No. Look carefully: from his right eyebrow, which starts from an oval and has been drawn toward his closed, plaster eyelid like a stroke in charcoal, a comet, or a calligrapher's initial, there is a large drop of blood falling, a trickle that descends, fed by its tiny source, faster now, along his cheek, down his wide neck; it runs across his torso and scores his waist and thigh, dividing the champion's lacerated effigy in asymmetrical parts for a class in acupuncture."

Scar

Like steam from a urinal, the cloying, tepid, slow swell of the fourth beer works its way through the body, oily and turbid. According to Lezama, that fourth dose of hops drove the Greeks mad.

Madness, or the fleeting suppression of loneliness, the foolish interruption of one's isolation: something sparks a kind of dialogue — actually a recurring soliloquy of a lyrical nature, both misty and vulgar — the turbanned man in rags who happens to be beside you at the bar, or the one swathed in the Spartan outfit of an amateur karate freak, or the one wearing a soiled white djellabah crisscrossed with embroidery in a different shade of white, and burn marks, and tears crudely darned. These daily disguises, mediocre simulacra of the sexual marketplace or of the fascinating erotic display of animals, arc abetted by the yellowish robes they hand us, with the solemnity of one presenting a scroll, at the entrance to the Moorish bathhouse that today will be officially abandoned to the rubble — to the ruins, both the Arabic arches and the Saharan landscapes that fill them.

In such transvestisms, which mimic winter fashions as well, and even the latest wretched vices of some Japanese sewing room, we all huddled together around the low tables, sheltered by the flickering pink light of the neon arcs.

Today, in this closure and enclosure, the beer's cloying brings to the surface, like a corpse in a swollen river, the precise memory, the minimal gesture that once saved us from the same solitude: the gravitation of a paternal gaze.

—

I was on my way home in the leaden noon that preceded the hailstorm the evening before the hurricane; the narrow, mud-covered streets and uneven mossy sidewalks of the village where I was born.

The swampy greenish water outside the cities

already held in its reflections, off in the distance, the façades of old colonial mansions whose beiges and ochres had been eaten away by humidity and neglect; the useless tower of some sugar refinery; and a withered, tuftless royal palm. Closer, those reflections caught the heavy boughs of a ceiba propped up by stakes as if they were tired or thirsty. A throng of mangy, low-flying turkey buzzards cawed in alarm at a nearby snake.

The house, which my father had wrested from a brackish and inopportune spring that gushed at dawn from the foundation, was sinking along a whitewashed hallway toward a patio filled with large earthenware jugs and refreshed by the red shadow of a royal poinciana. The noise of a nearby sawmill and the smell of glue and damp wood were cast into a dense bluish well amidst the mottled motion of the branches. In the morning, the goldfish poisoned by the glue fumes floated on the small pond, iridescent and open-mouthed.

I was riding my bicycle along the hallway, from the drawing room to the patio, when the pain shot through me. Appendicitis: the crude semiotics of our local medicine did not hesitate for a moment. To take me to the Colonia Española, a hospital that glimmered in a cloud of dust in the middle of a palm grove, complete with minarets and covered with friezes and ornamental tiles, we hired a car that appeared at dawn, piercing the mist with its yellow lights.

A medical mosque, the Colonia was a labyrinth of tile-paved rooms, tropical gardens, chapels, and operating theaters. On the marble shelves of the pharmacy, greenish liquids of different densities and viscosities were lined up in ornate bottles; when the Basque pharmacist handled them, they shone with a fishy, poisonous glitter.

Such was the rocky ground I covered before the operation as I strolled in the white gown of the confined, with my pubes like a Mohammedan's and my armpits thoroughly shaved. My body seemed like a continent to me, an opaque, fragile container always quick to break: a glass overflowing with viscera.

I also understood the paternal gaze — I had seen his hidden weeping as they took me to the hospital — it was a protection, a caring that enveloped, *the substance of a suture.*

I knew that his gaze, applied to my body as if

with a brush — Lacan — would protect me my whole life.

—

I evoked it then, in the solitude of that last afternoon in the bathhouse, amidst the embalming steam of the hammam, where, just as long ago in the island clinic, we had all gathered for the last time beneath the Mozarabic arches, sheathed in our linen robes, emaciated and already nostalgic.

The lights were turned off.

A dilapidated, twangy clock struck six as best it could.

We ordered the last beer.

His face hidden in a heap of dirty towels, his back to the room, the owner was weeping.

Two Broken Uppers,
a Stitch in My Lower Lip, or
Christ on the Rue Jacob

It all began in the United States, at Princeton University. An ordinary accident, a slip in the snow — the truth is, there was no snow — only an ambiguous game with a student imperfectly ignorant of judo. He had believed in my alcoholic, nocturnal simulation — I roughed out a karate dance — and had me in a swift lock so suddenly I landed on the ground.

After I spent a night with my face covered by ice, the way corpses are packed in dry ice, they decided to take me to the hospital so I could get some stitches to repair my lips.

That was the start of my American death, the pause that refreshes. What was happening? I had no idea. That Sunday morning, a dozen doctors and nurses, red-eyed like sleepwalkers, were dealing with their patients in total exhaustion. They pulled Coke after Coke from a soda machine; at times their pale-green uniforms and their masks turned them into a team of astronauts adrift under the neon lights, at times they were like contrite penitents framing a grave.

The hospital cubicles were divided by thin curtains of transparent plastic. You could hear perfectly everything going on in the next cubicle, and you could even make out the gestures of an emergency operation, although they were blurred and seemed to occur in slow motion.

I could hear through the dirty transparency of the curtain: "I wonder if she'll die." Someone, without the least formality, the way you request a piece of simple information, was inquiring about death.

—

As I was leaving, duly sutured, I immediately recognized in the distance the low voices punctuated by sobs and shouts I had heard so often in Black churches when I was a child.

The sanctuary of the church where they took me, near the hospital, was jammed. These Sunday worshipers were obviously fond of loud colors, shunning the facile discretion of grays: elaborate hot-pink hats, pistachio-green dresses, shoes in lacquered Japanese red with high platforms, a few pearly feathers fluttering with the movement of purple nails and gold eyelids.

In this congregation layered with makeup, talking to God was all a strident shout of protest, an act of excess. They roared with laughter, they cried, they repeated the minister's words as if they were in a trance, while he demanded that God grant some request immediately, using the oratorical emphasis and exaggerated, grandiloquent gestures of a South American caudillo, speaking to a surly, English, bullying God, threatening Him with something, or pleading with Him to explain His absence on a particular occasion, His levity, or His indifference.

"Yes," these Protestants shouted, "that's true!"

And they kept crying and chanting.

—

I was drinking an ice-cold beer in the Pré-aux-clercs, at the corner of Jacob and Bonaparte, in Paris.

Suddenly traffic stopped to make way for a large open truck. It was delivering a painting as large as a house to some church or to the nearby Louvre. The painting was rounded at the top, as if it were going to be hung in a specific place, between two columns and under an arch. It portrayed the scourging of Christ, who was contemplating the Rue Jacob, the bar, perhaps even my ice-cold beer.

I understood immediately that he was trying to tell me something — Christ, or rather, Painting, which has always spoken to me. Or perhaps, instead, I wanted to tell him something. Yes, that's how it was.

I wanted to tell him forcefully, in the same tone used by the black minister at Princeton University. I wanted to tell him something in that tone, I'm sure of it. But I never found out what.

Omphalos

"All scars," François Wahl notes as he finishes his reading of my short inventory of marks made on skin, "refer to a single scar: the first one, the umbilical excision, the only invisible scar."

If that scar, sunk now in the small circular labyrinth that centers my belly, the erased signature of my birth, comes into the slightest contact with anything, I feel ill. My own fingers as I bathed, the clumsy lips of a lover have at times erred in Eros and offered the casual caress that led to nausea. Perhaps this explains my reluctance to evoke that scar, the intensity of the silence that seals off my entry into the world, my miraculous access to breath, to air.

My mother inherited her inductive talent from my maternal grandmother, a skillful Camagüeyan midwife. She also inherited my grandmother's clairvoyance; this meant that she could foretell a disastrous delivery, an imminent accident, or, just before the herald's arrival, the swat of death's paw; and with an inflection so natural, it seemed an indication of absolute certainty.

I don't know if that premonition assisted at her first delivery: I was born choking.

The umbilical cord cut with one slash, the robust tribal African midwife held the screamless child by his feet. She shook him like a bunch of small sweet bananas, as if to loosen the ripe ones or frighten away a *sijú,* that nocturnal bird of prey. Nothing. The new mother was eagerly awaiting the bruised howl that would attest to her fertility, but the batch of nerves, the squashed ideogram of quivering little bones was not about to give even the smallest indication of its existence.

Four slaps on the behind, accompanied by Yoruban harangues against the lazy *orishas,** made me emit my first stridence, the bellowing scream that a fashionable tautology describes as "primal."

---

*Afro-Cuban deities. (Trans. note.)

His body hoisted like a bloody trophy, a fetish of placental thread, the screamer's scar began to contract, shrinking into the umbilical labyrinth, the bonding of dried fibrils, until it disappeared below the surface and was hidden in the pores, in the archaeology of his skin.

This explains my shivers when anything comes in contact with that scar. It's like the threat of being choked, like the return of a silence that preceded screams and air, a silence that must be identical to the other one, to the final silence that follows our birth in reverse.

A Wart on My Foot

I got to S.'s studio early in the morning so I could see his latest work before it went off to Los Angeles. He opened the gate for me fully dressed; he was even wearing a shirt and tie at that hour, his blond hair shining as if he had just oiled it. I knew immediately that something was wrong. Gesturing impatiently, he shooed away a menacing dog that seemed about to take a bite out of me.

"I'm fine," he said right away, his tone that of someone engaged in an extended conversation. "C.'s the one who's in bad shape. His friend G. has been on an IV for a week."

With an assurance contradicted by something in his voice, he walked toward the studio like an actor who has finished his lines.

The human body is a machine held upright by a system of hinges. My hinges opened and broke apart. I stood there rigidly, leaning against a radiator, as if the heat could keep me standing, strengthen my spine. I fixed my gaze on S.'s paintings as on a bull's-eye; there, in fact, the human body is trapped in an irregular oval. It tries to put itself back together, to magnetize the fragments dislocated and dispersed by the flash of color. Parkinsoned by the chromatic discharge, those huge Gardelian* dolls shake and take flight toward a charcoal sky.

As I looked at them, I understood my reaction. I understood what my body was telling me: AIDS is a stalking. It feels as if someone, at any moment, under any pretext at all, could knock on the door and carry you off forever, as if an undetermined danger hovered in the air and could solidify, jell in the space of an instant. Who will be next? For how long will you escape? Everything gathers the weight of a threat. The Jews, it seems, know this feeling well.

—

After a quick glance, the nonchalant nurse who was attending to me said the best thing would be to

*After Carlos Gardel, the legendary tango singer. (Trans. note.)

remove the wart surgically, because it had grown so large and so deep, even though it was barely visible on the sole of my foot.

A few hours later I was on the table and the doctor took my blood pressure, asked me if I'd had any anesthetic yet, gave me an injection, made the first incisions.

"Do you feel anything?" he said.

"Nothing," I replied, with the certainty that handling microphones has taught me to feign.

"Or, yes," I added immediately, "I do have a feeling that . . . but this has nothing to do with what's going on here. That there's something burning outside. Smells like burnt rubber."

"It's not outside," he answered, but without looking at me, concentrating on his meticulous task, "and it's not rubber. I've already removed the wart and now I'm cauterizing your skin. What you smell is singed human flesh."

"We Jews," he added without the slightest change in his expression, "are very familiar with this smell."

II
LESSONS IN THE EPHEMERAL

Unity of Place

The tourist brochures are always right. As proof, this sentence found in a pink flyer with blurred letters: "You will leave Benares, but Benares will not leave you. Something deep inside you will have changed forever." It would be difficult to put that any better or give a more satisfactory answer to the question that comes up before each trip back to India: Why go to Benares to meditate if you can meditate anywhere? Or, to ask the question another way: Isn't there more silence just about anywhere else, fewer aggressive, maniacal monkeys, fewer lepers grabbing at your shirt with their long fingers eaten by pink sores?

In fact, only one difference can be cited between Benares and some supposed utopian landscape. On the banks of the Ganges, what thinks is the space itself. There, men and things emit signs, as if a certain sense ran through them, as if they were shaken by a force that belonged to the divine or the demonic. The nearness of this force is marked by something resembling an incandescence, as if the unspeakable were burning. Not real-life men but personages, who parade naked, their skin inscribed with Sanskrit writings, or wrapped in vast golden saris. In this parade, which occurs after their death, they have been covered with white flowers: their stretchers cross the noisy urban crush of cows and trucks toward the bonfire, held aloft by the faithful who cannot help brushing them against the windows of buses, flooding the buses with their lethal perfume.

Legend has it that Varanasi — the real name of Benares — was the first city of the world, built by time as well as by man. The Hindus believe that if you die on the proper side of the Ganges, you can enjoy a considerable reduction, maybe even an exemption, from the inevitable price implicit in reincarnation; the other bank of the river, avoided by everyone at all cost, is regressive and nefarious. Buddhists insist that before he went to preach his first sermon, near the gazelles in the neighboring park of Sarnath, the Buddha Sakyamuni, who at that point had renounced all excess — both stubborn austerity and enjoyment eventually become tedious — crossed the city in silence. Some litter was left to mark his passage through Islam, and his iconoclastic followers then retired discreetly. As for Christianity, it is so present today that the popular icons that have made the printers of Bombay world famous include not only Ganesha, the playful, candy-eating elephant god, but also a meticulously made-up Christ encircled by an iridescent halo. At the center of such engravings, without the slightest theological resentment, the ideal couple from the Indian pantheon, Shiva and Parvati, shine with kitsch's pearly patina.

The essential thing is a dip in the Ganges, although it makes little difference which god receives the honor of your dedication. At 6 A.M. fanaticism convinces one that those waters, still opaque with ashes from last evening's incinerators, are transparent and fresh.

I rent one of the pirated, hollowed-out canoes that traverse the river near the ghats. I get in with my companion, and at the center of the stream I throw the neatly typed manuscript of one of my novels into the water. The astonished boatman asks me in his soprano-voiced British English if it's a sacred book.

Predictable result: the millennial waters do not accept my "offering." The boxed manuscript floats, drifts, does not sink, and, what is worse, begins to make its gradual way back to the evil shore. The three of us, philosopher, boatman, and rejected author, follow the ill-fated text over the waters, and we charge after it, paddling furiously. Until the current carries it off. Toward the delta, toward god.

Three immersions: by Brahma, by Shiva, by Vishnu. Ochre stretches behind the faithful and the stone steps running down to the shore: porous earth, walls, wood, the wicker of umbrellas covered with red letters. On the façades of old colonial palaces in ruins, the Party's didactic emblem is repeated like a mockery or the flip side of so much mysticism. The sky is ochre too, from smoke and ash. A motionless flight of crows.

—

Benares is not a city but a border: one of the borders of the Ganges. It is also the border of the Earth, since these waters are said to communicate directly with heaven. The river is the double — or the reflection — of another, invisible river, which flows in another space, in a time without time, and its source coincides with the source of all possible creation, including the creation of the illusion we call reality.

Only one of the borders is habitable; the other, by metaphysical decree, has been relegated to condemnation and invisibility. English canoes, pallid and peeling, monkey temples, bonfires, and barges are amassed on the permitted bank; on the ground interminable strips of cloth have been spread after being beaten on the rocks. Seen from above, the parallel bands of black, gold, vermilion, and burnt orange outline something like the symbol of a good omen that precedes one's ritual immersion.

The opposite shore also communicates with something invisible, with an *ailleurs,* an elsewhere, but an infernal one. This explains why it is always deserted. The devotees abandon it at the least sign of approaching death; to die there — at night the only things left are sick, demented, and untouchable animals — means a fatal setback in the inexorable karmic progression. Compared to that, any physical transformation must represent an advancement.

The good border attracts as much as the other border repels. Thousands of pilgrims arrive daily from all over India, tormented and anemic, thirsty for the only water that washes, the only water that cleanses and liberates, in spite of its persistent cloudiness. At night, tiny flames flit over that water, minute oil lamps amidst wilted, one-rupee flowers that adorn the prescribed offerings deposited in unstable wicker rings.

Some of the pilgrims live under the umbrellas on the bank, with no belongings except a Sanskrit manuscript, a few paintbrushes, and a large copper cup. With the help of the small mirror from a compact, a young saddhu undertakes the true work of a copyist. Beginning at dawn, millimeter by millimeter, he transcribes on his skin, which he has previously covered with ashes as if it were a page, letters from a small piece of dusty palm wood full of holes, an illegible board. As if the last possible interpretation must pass through the torture of dermal reproduction, or as if each human body has access to meaning only when transformed into a moving text, into a deciphering and inscription.

A little higher up on the steps, toward the city, under a tattered canopy, Durga's robust followers have been singing uninterruptedly, with a microphone and loudspeaker, for the last nine days.

Dark-browed and smiling, with fiercely drawn features and a red dot placed in the center of her forehead, dancing and graceful, the pink celluloid goddess waves her multiple arms, while with her left foot she squashes a small chubby-cheeked demon with knowing eyes who accepts his sentence merrily, never ceasing to play his ritual pipe.

Two circles of little blinking lightbulbs in all colors halo the victim and the disagreeable divinity.

Monsoon heat. The smell of spices. Pyramidal mounds of vermilion, cinnabar, violet, mustard yellow, green, and white dust pressed by hand. In the dense air the small bells, tambourines, and the crashing of a gong from one of Benares's two thousand temples reverberate a few instants before fading in the buzz of the crowd. Someone is crying. Truculent yogis compete on their beds of spikes. A corpse passes, wrapped in silver brocade, like a mummy in its humid bandages. A white-faced monkey — mask of Kathakali — with its swollen red behind flies furiously between two golden towers. Someone is putting makeup on a little boy: an enormous conical hat, countless necklaces of yellow flowers, as proof of caste. He is gobbling a fluorescent, helicoid ice cream.

Deep and dark, the shops smell of cinnamon. There are heaps of small wooden statues, flashy bracelets, rainbow silks, a sitar, and even some recently manufactured mandalas. Behind the shops is the Viswanatha, where only Hindus are permitted. Its tower is overlaid with gold. In the center of the great room — visible from a neighboring balcony, if one pays for the privilege — there is a magnificently powerful, arrogant, almost boastful erection. No other word is adequate: it is a gigantic lingam, Shiva's symbolic phallus, fount of all energy, all possible action.

The crowd adores it so emphatically that for the hurried Westerner the temple is nothing but a poorly dissimulated perversion. He leaves it to follow a dusty highway filled with bicycles and cows, the route taken by a disillusioned prince from the Sakya clan on his journey to Sarnath five hundred years before our era. There, a bo tree, or gigantic fig, recalls the tree of Gaya; beneath it the Buddha received enlightenment when he was nothing more than Gautama. Part of that first sermon has been engraved on a stone. The words seem very straightforward and their content could be summarized in simple aphorisms; for example, how to follow the "middle road" throughout one's entire life, without excesses or errors. Still valid, the message is more timely today than it was when offered before five attentive monkeys and a few gazelles. It will be so until the coming of Maitreya.

If in fact Benares never does leave us because of the violence of its color, because of its uncontrollable proliferation of gods and things, Sarnath, on the other hand — as one would expect in Buddhism — captures visitors with its silence, with that borderless void bounded only by two stupas, or funeral tumuli in ruins, and the prayer wheels of some Tibetan monks in exile. The afternoon wind rustles the leaves of the bo tree, and the faithful gather them as thcy fall.

Always visited together and in haste, the two

cities six miles apart are like the two possible images of a single thought. One thought, disguised by the word, conceives reality as pure simulacrum; the other has understood, from the beginning and irreversibly, that the void pierces everything and that the perceptible whole is nothing other than its metaphor or its emanation.

Some rhetorical figure, whichever prompts the greatest closeness, will allow me to state that Henri Le Saux set out from here.

Actually, I am writing in the Oise River region of France, and Henri Le Saux left a Benedictine monastery in Brittany.

His proximity — a different proximity — is inseparable, however, from that of this landscape, from what surrounds us. A desire perhaps, a thirst we had in the past but which left us, has been set aside — this is the pretext for all banishments — because of work: the thirst for the origin, for the absolute beginning, for that place in thought whence there is no return.

Christianity, I think he thought — although here "to think" is not merely an approximating verb —

was too focused on a single presence, and besides too total, too unmediated. He wanted to dissolve into totality, into a proliferation of all colors and all things, or into that thought in which all things have the same dimension, the same depth — from the basalt lingam deep in a humid shrine, gleaming in the night, covered with coins and petals, spewing its milky fluid, to the shadow cast by a leaf on a red wall, or the barking of a dog in the distance.

Then — but temporal adverbs are more than inadequate in this research, or in this search — dissolution into everything manifest, into everything endowed with appearance, was no longer enough for him.

He wanted to stop being; he sought annihilation, sought to suppress even the idea of an "I," to reach a silence so absolute that there would be no one capable of verifying his existence: no observer for that nothingness.

If there is no listening — I feel he felt — then there is no subject.

He wanted — and this is how he expressed it, as he traveled the dusty roads of India like a beggar — to be *wearing space.*

That journey led him perhaps to pure divinity; certainly to the headstreams of the Ganges, that is, to the roof of the world. Or to madness.

In the Socco Chico, the Medicine Plaza in Tangier, Roland Barthes identified the "site of writing." What are the coordinates of that site?

Spain, seen there "from below," functions as a magnetic north both utopian and close. It is seen from an outside, from things that have been rejected, expelled, things that still bear the indelible mark and the archaeology of that separation. To negotiate those arabesques — in the most literal sense of the term — to travel that edge implies nothing less than to reread, from the place of things that have been repressed and censored, an initial condition of Spanishness. Here, however, Spanishness is read inside out, against the current, from the night of its adversary. Like the Spain depicted by Juan Goytisolo in *Don Julián* (Count Julian), this Spain is circumscribed in a curious phonetic mirror, and the object of that circumscription is none other than the object of circumcision.

Stereophony of the Socco Chico: the ground slopes; the plaza has an ear in two cities. Voices overridden by the ever-present voice of Oum Kalsoum. Djellabahs are reflected on the smooth stones, after the rain. At the Koranic school small sopranos begin to sing suras. Tiny spoons stirring basil leaves in cups of hot cloying tea. Other languages, but spoken in hoarse voices, from Santander or Andalusia; a Castilian so ethereal that mouth means ear and ear nose . . .

An entire stereophony of torn posters adorns the plaza. Still dripping, the Arabic characters drawn with tar by someone in the night mix with the remains of Latin typography. Stripes, wide mobile bands like those on the linen djellabahs; striped figures: light filters through the wicker roof over a narrow covered street. Indigo: on the sand, frayed parallel rectangles of carpet glimmer at midday. Orange: the ceiling of a bar depicts a revolving, star-studded sky with sudden dawns. In the swaying of tarnished copper lamps, layers of smoke mix with green swirls of mint, ginger, a whiff of hash and rum.

In the Meridian cemetery, the shadows cast by cones wrapped in Kufic bands lengthen with the day on the rough stones; their reverse is a large saffron spot shifting across the ornamental tiles on the floor at Manolo's house. A plank of palm slides, obscuring a large lantern with cracked yellow panes. When it opens, one glimpses for a moment the faces in the waiting room, the soldiers' coarse outfits, a flame lighting a cigar.

Polygons studded with stars. The neon light around the plaster domes flickers. Bakelite mihrab. Polyester latticework.

Drague, or cruising, and drugs: the façades circling the plaza in the cool of the shade appear to be perforated, honeycombed with holes; some holes are small — dwelling cubicles or cafés — others expand into a network of dark corridors, mustard-colored hallways, and rooms smelling of starch. "Gilt and red plush. Rococo bar backed by pink shell. The air is cloyed with a sweet evil substance like decayed honey. Men and women in evening dress sip poussecafés through alabaster tubes. A Mugwump sits naked on a bar stool covered in pink silk. He licks warm honey from a crystal goblet with a long black tongue. His genitals are perfectly formed — circumcised cock, black shiny pubic hairs. Mugwump push a slender blond youth to a couch and strip him expertly. He draws back a silk curtain to reveal a wooden scaffold in the middle of a platform covered with Aztec tiles, in front of a luminous screen of red quartz . . . At that time I was living in one room in the Native Quarter of Tangier. My Spanish friends called me El Hombre Invisible — the Invisible Man." (William Burroughs, *Naked Lunch*, Tangier, 1959.)

Because It's Real

THE STRATAGEM OF THE TICK

The tick, said Roland Barthes — who extracted the information from God knows what libertine manual of entomology — waits sometimes for years, clinging to the branch of a tree in a state of slumber, or slightly comatose, till a coveted hot-blooded animal passes below.

Then he leaps, immediately and blindly, with the infallible aim of instinct, and burrows into the skin of his prey until he dies, puffed up and glutted with that warm black jelly, his wait finally satiated.

—

After twenty years of loyal service to the company — as they say in that despicable jargon — and of a fidelity close to adulation or penitence, some clumsy paperwork leads me to commit a minor error.

"Finally," the little boss calls me in, all puffed up, "I caught you red-handed!"

As if I were a confirmed bungler, an opportunist, a rogue.

How long had he been waiting, clinging, for the smell of blood?

For many years, twenty perhaps, we went to the same café. This could be a narrative in the past tense, but it actually occurs in the present: we continue to go, though no longer in the mood, almost out of duty, simply to repeat a routine that is becoming more and more infrequent.

I can date my first encounter with Saint-Germain des Près to 1957 in Camagüey, Cuba, plowing through the concise pages of a philosophy manual that supported current morality, no doubt to give it an air of truth. This didactic study lamented that the Quartier, overrun by an existentialist furor or outright seediness, flaunted so much decorum that it was indecent; the dark exposure of a photograph of the Flore, in stern sepia, corroborated the author's premises.

The second contact was subterranean. We were
students, plain and simple. A recent popular revolution and a scholarship had led us to this cultured
and damp river city. We were inaugurating our
heavy gray coats as well as the surprise or phobia
occasioned by a Metro ride, the changing trees,
Gallicisms, and snow.

Entangled in the underground lines, I discovered
that a central station bore the name of this zone I
had assumed was off-limits, or in the outskirts, con-
demned by the manual to some bucolic province.

That same night I sought out the Flore.

Because of the prestige I have always conferred
upon mythologies and "brand-name" images (their
audiovisual avatars) — I never question the catalogue
of excellent qualities a convincing announcer recites
about any product — it took me years to discover the
Flore. On the other hand I persuaded the then recep-
tive Roland Barthes, years back, to join me after
dinner in Pigalle, which guaranteed him the pica-
resque pleasantries of those burlesque shows in the
north (according to my expanded geography of the
city). Of the many places solicited or vindicated by
the all-embracing adjective *gay,* the Flore, retaining

such a label with interest, is the place that least warrants it; there are no encounters, or only sporadic ones: chilly, fleeting, and combative.

Fugitives from Cinecittà's shabby studios careened there — and here I speak of the redundant Romans or even Yugoslavs from those Greco-Latin soap operas in black and white that employed thousands of naked and plumed warriors with a single exterior set. Having achieved the decisive and irascible "bit part" articulated before a languid star, these benevolent extras in their fly-by-night studios aspired to the director, who would serve, each day less probably, as their trampoline — the metaphor is a quotation — amid repeated Helvetian broths in soluble cubes, unlabeled wine bottles with plastic corks, stale cheese preserved by the open air, and synthetic leopardskin bedspreads, or, indistinguishable from them, the authentic leopard skins in the Negresco suites during the film festival.

The salon at twilight was also magnetized, more than once, by the eyes of "La Luna." Her emerald contact lenses dazzled in the stagnant and rainy air of autumn, adding yet another astral shine to those of her smooth skull and varnished skin. She reversed and redeemed the travels of her aforementioned col-leagues upon abandoning that cockroachy setting with a postwar air for the flaming Flavian baroque of the *Satyricon*.

From Fellini she went on to other trips. She came to believe, thanks to the ubiquity of overdoses, that just by desiring it she could dine once again in a makeshift eatery by the Trastevere and, with drunken descendants, in a fin de siècle castle on the outskirts of London. Her last lysergic supplement carried her off to death.

—

The facile trope is valid: the Flore has its fauna: almost unremovable, cloying regulars. The café's mutating stars, flattered or deferred to with perse-vering sarcasm and equal intensity by dynastic clans and rivalrous servile fans, can be cited: Marcel Carné — on the terrace, to the right, bedecked by film archaeologists and a Légion d'Honneur button; David Hockney — white plastic eyeglasses, drawings under his arm; Andy Warhol — albino wig and sepulchral pallor; Jorge Semprún — the morning cof-fee is not what it used to be, nor the croissants;

Francis Bacon — in the back, at the table of *Being and Nothingness* by pure chance; Roland Barthes — with his eyes fixed on *Le Monde* — he would feign an interest that shooed away admirers and intruders; and, to join him and reiterate aperitifs, François Wahl and myself.

The rank and file of the Flore, however — I'm resorting to labor union dialect — became invisible in their persistence. An American painter was a morbid curio for suburban and habitual affiliates: she sat sallow and emaciated, her nails and lips painted the same black, beside her tiny and fluently sententious dog — had he been amid red coffers and flyswatters, he could have adorned a Chinese silk painting — both mummified before a cup of coffee, like two Egyptian chancellors before an ibis.

A disheveled and diabolical accordionist called Cui-Cui, a relic immune to invasions and rationings who pretended to play on the sidewalk a bucolic milonga,* inhabited by parrots whose cries — hence her nickname — were imitated, and with such precision, by her madness. Unless madness is not precisely that stagy simulation: feigning madness.

*Argentine dance music. (Trans. note.)

Plus: writers ragged and ecological, recycling the names of dead men, fans of white wine and science fiction; flamboyant black transvestites, with their excessive earrings and tailored suits, always hiding a yawn and seen in profile; the nouveau poor in working class jeans; opulent though honest bureaucrats; amateur drug dealers; and many interchangeable, well-groomed gays, pompous with their chalk faces and aluminum eyelids, and at the same time abusive precursors, slaves and terrorists of winter fashion, ready for any torture induced by laconic advertisements, *dazibaos* urgently scribbled on the walls of the W.C., or sectarian and sarcastic, dressed according to the latest *Vogue*'s unnameable dicta, and for whom the shy or the prudent — démodé and cheap, as far as they're concerned — continue modeling last year's shameful apparel.

In the Flore I discovered the Bloody Mary, whose initial proportions (tomato juice with vodka) would be inverted with the years by my innate sybaritism — in my first restaurant, barely a schoolboy, I ordered a dish of my own invention, as nonexistent as it was exquisite: fried chicken brains — or by the justifiable shrewdness of waiters who, mocking a maitre's almost panoptic vigilance, double the dose of alcohol with careless and scrupulously forgetful gestures, in a glass which, suspended with orthogonal and mechanical movements — a quotation from futurism — at the top of the bottle, after the citric and frozen alchemy of the bar and from the comprehensive counter — a Pop quotation — would reach my hand with ornate courtesies.

I first drank to be festive, out of a provincial sense of splendor, yielding to a naive parvenu luxury; then, for a year, to throttle with the foggy and vulgar shield of alcohol, like a familiar and cheap Chinese screen, the meanness of a word, the betrayal of a pact; finally, out of boredom, to catch a fleeting adjective from mere repetition.

The revolution of alcohol — in the astronomical sense of the term, like that of a planet always obeying its orbit, immutable and regular — lends itself to an infallible and comfortable prognosis, to the prediction of pedestrian and categorical repetitions.

Alcohol either attenuates or provokes a substantiation: all is empty, or — there's a generous certainty in synonyms, in this case its most hackneyed and now depreciated — anguish. Soon one becomes excessive, socially and chemically maladjusted, neglecting both the body and protocol. This hysterical excess and theatricality, always aggressive or submissive, distant or tearful, talkative or taciturn, repulses the abstemious, but in the drinker's murky code its expression is quite moderate and legitimate: a precise, rigorous, lucid, and barely exterior monologue.

Then, out of shame or sheer will power, as if obeying an unformulated threat or self-punishment — entreaties and reprimands, more than ineffective, are noxious — a brutal severing, astringency, an orgy of water.

For a month. Or two. Until the seed of a deceptive security is sown, a mistaken sense of self-sufficiency: "I am capable of stopping, I can do what I wish, I have proven it to myself. Therefore, why deprive myself of this pleasure, if life is so short? Of course I shall drink in moderation, etc." And on to the next drink. The first of the new revolution, a star in orbit.

—

G. Bateson, in *Steps to an Ecology of the Mind,* is the only one who has formulated alcohol's unremitting progression in terms that avoid the subject's lengthy and constructive bibliography, the hodge-podge of hygienic discourse and the mediocre charisma of normaloid moralizing. He shifts the attention of the thirsty from the period of absorption upon which common sense has focused, to the period of continence, which for him is equally alcoholic; continence is an antipodal lover and false counterpoint of its opposite, as well as a condition and a fragment of its orbit. He preserves many premises of his predecessors, though not the impertinent use of will power: futile to resort to that Pharisaical ally. He emphasizes, rather, its corruption and deterioration.

The repetition of alcohol, its pacifying compulsion, is not alien to those who cherish ritual, especially in that tedious or insane variation that is the uninterrupted utterance of a mantra: some monks, throughout their lives, do not allow recess in the exercise of *Om mani padme hum*. Others, Western novices accustomed to income-yielding instruments, add up a prescribed computation of diamonds and lotus flowers, guarantees of programmed illumination in such fiscal Buddhism.

Nothing has crossed my exile that does not

reach its best definition in that word: repetition. *Obsessions, rituals, writings.* I could include the cyclical work of phobia; also painting, a pastoral Sunday ritual, if the voluntary recurrence of the same paint stroke saturating a vast and defenseless surface is gratifying. And even *la drague,* that expectant and punitive cruising — in a Dantesque inferno, lovers against nature cruising through eternity, as if the punishment for that insubordination were no more than the monstrous or metaphysical multiplication of its propitious rite: running after an object perhaps more fleeting than the others, confirming, once it's reached, the border that separates it from the phantom, almost enjoying precisely that lapse, that difference, and setting off in pursuit of yet another.

The drive toward repetition is, it would seem, also a property of death. The demise of one's everyday friend is present, then, not in his empty place at the Flore, nor in the daily unconscious wait for him, but in repetition's rituals which designate and invoke him. In the obsession of the reiterated and detestable Bloody Mary, in erotic rituals. In writing.

This morning, in the country, an almost autumn day. Depressed about not yet feeling on vacation, far from the sea, far from those I love — according to Sei Shonagon, the Japanese courtesan who catalogued everything, this is the real reason for most unhappiness — I head for the woods in search of dialogue, or to relieve the sexual dreams that assault me nightly with their incoherence and pollutions.

In the woods — remembering San Juan de la Cruz — two deer pass quickly, frightened. I wait in the car, drinking a can of beer. Nothing.

As I'm about to leave, a truck appears, white and enormous like a spaceship or a futurist machine. Through the complex reflections of the rearview mirrors and the mournful glow of autumn, I see what's happening. The truck driver gets out: blond, stocky, about thirty years old. I get out of the car too. He looks at me.

He opens a door at the back of the truck — a kind of ramp or medieval drawbridge. He looks at me again from inside. Without the slightest hesitation I leave my car and jump into the truck. The automatic door closes slowly, with a screech.

He looks at me again, but without saying a word. We open our flies and begin to masturbate each other. The truck — I now realize — transports dirty laundry. It's loaded with metal baskets which look like monkey cages, filled with sheets, tablecloths, pillowcases from God knows what leprosarium or hospital, white uniforms impregnated with wine, perforated by burns, by dark bloody stains. We lick each other's penis only very lightly — no doubt for fear of AIDS. Finally, now on the verge of ejaculation, we kiss.

Nothing is said. It strikes me that he must be Polish, or German — the highway irrigates all of Europe. I don't think he speaks French.

With the same finger he uses to close his fly he presses a button at the center of a control panel and opens the door of the truck.

"Everything okay?" I ask.

"*Ça va*" is his only answer.

I go out into the light, into the day of the deer, now sure of being really clean.

Unity of Figure

ETHEJUNGLETHEJUNGLETHEJUNGLETHEJUN
GLETHEJUNGLETHEJUNGLETHEJUNGLETH
EJUNGLETHEJUNGLETHEJUNGLETHEJUN
GLETHEJUNGLETHEJUNGLETHEJUNGLETH
EJUNGLETHEJUNGLETHEJUNGLETHEJUN
GLETHEJUNGLETHEJUNGLETHEJUNGLETHE
JUNGLETHEJUNGLETHEJUNGLETHE
GLETHEJUNGLETHEJUN
JUNGLETHEJUNGLETHEJUNGLETH

THE JUNGLE

Everything straight — tubes of sugarcane, long knee-
less legs, cylinders that serve as arms — breaks into a
curve: buttocks, liana, hammock, the path across the
sky followed by the diurnal moon.

Everything is ephemeral, like a flock in flight,
although fixed nevertheless, motionless in the dense
air, in the island stillness of midday.

But no: a slight shiver, a swaying, green and
white, in the yagruma tree's swollen leaves, in the
robust blossoms dripping a transparent purple slime,
in the red lines of the viny trunks. Something is
moving, something is happening: the wind, the escape of a fugitive slave, the threat of open scissors.
Large flat feet stomp the ground.

It's the laughing gods, wearing small horned
masks, shaking their horsehair mops, the asymmetry

of herons drawn with a single line; the lesser gods who inhabit the jungle, the mischievous ones with their famous little voices that sound like damp drums. The playful gods who go their way, indifferent to the calls of men, or bored, or fed up with miracles, or sarcastic, or clumsy.

The sleepwalkers go off, then, leaving nothing in the canebrake but their signatures, their emblems of painted wood and guano, empty simulacra.

They're off, to amuse themselves with the mulatto women, to eat ripe *caimitos,* to dance until they collapse — let men get by however they can — their bodies inscribed with saffron scribbles.

They've gone: off to the mountains.

What a mess! It's been at least a week since anyone has swept or even picked up the cigarette butts. Not to mention the waste of electricity: all the lights are on in broad daylight.

Everything in that hopping shantytown dive, or in that rural shack, is negligence, oblivion, absence of law.

Only the little girl, reduced by a symbolic perspective to the status of skittish dwarf, clinging to those splendid skirts, and the bulldog in the foreground wearing something that looks like a saddle, indifferent to the exotic apples, sense the imminence of danger: the row that will ensue once the theft is discovered.

That's the party, our party: fusion, relatives bound fast in a space beyond all prohibition. Fumbling clum-

sily, the Sapphic servant pulls a fast one on the potbel-
lied drunk who in turn works fast — Saint Anne, the
Virgin, and the Christ child — with the robust Venus.
The arms of the offshoots, in Botero's family portraits,
blend with the branches of the orange tree that shade
his groups, among plump pigeons.

A total blast. In the air there's a suggestion of
colonial guitars, maracas, and frosty beer. Their
mahogany-daubed locks glistening with Glostora
and swaying to the music, the houris swing their
hips wildly, opening their lips exuberantly, saying
yes with a bat of their purple eyelids. Flimsy pink or
greenish patent-leather shoes sparkle next to crush-
ing rustic high-top boots.

A total blast? Look at the eyes of the drunk with
the loosened tie. A mortuary fiesta: our baroque is
funereal.

A sadness from before time, from before the
Conquest and before language clouded our siesta
and our binge, as if a candied little dead woman
with a twangy, nasal voice were shouting behind the
singers and guitarists: Enjoy, enjoy!

The characters are bound fast, as in a Laocoön,
but each one is trapped in loneliness.

No one looks at anyone else.

There's an extra hand, holding a glass.

The Gulf of Morbihan, in Brittany, takes the unprepared tourist by surprise because the area is covered with megalithic monuments: rows or alignments of standing stones, more than 2,500 in total, some of them up to four meters tall.

The alignment of the stones at regular intervals began long before the Egyptian pyramids were built, when the first farmers settled in this region in 5000 BC.

The Carnac alignment is located near the hamlet of Le Ménec. As evidenced by the walls of the large houses there today, the village inhabitants soon found a practical use for the stones, which had a solely mythic significance when the monuments were erected. There are 1,100 monuments and they stretch toward the northeast in twelve orderly avenues for one kilometer. The rows are not equidistant from each other; those along the edges are closer together. Although they appear to be parallel, in fact they converge toward the east, so that seen from an airplane, they form something that resembles a huge closed fan. Archaeologists claim there were 7,000 stones in Carnac when the twelve avenues were intact. At the end of the avenues are remains of a grouping of megaliths, but it is circular.

Postcard tourists use the alignments for horseback riding, and children decide right away that the place was invented for playing hide-and-seek. Others are possessed first by curiosity and then by uneasiness and even anxiety, because in the end the alignments, whose origin and function are unknown, amount to an enigma hurled to man today from the depths of time — a radical questioning or, to put it in less serious terms, a conundrum.

Archaeologists throughout the world continually venture hypotheses about the Nazca geoglyphics, the sculptures on Easter Island, or the pyramids in Egypt and Mexico. Nothing is known, however, nor does anyone venture to speak about the rows of megaliths at Carnac. Were they offerings made by the first farmers to the distant rain and sun gods? Were they used as a physical method of recording solar and lunar cycles to determine the time for each harvest? Were they an observatory? A site of ceremonies performed in order to mark the exact midpoint of winter and other important moments in the sun's journey? The tombs are almost always found close to the alignments; in one of them, Newgrange, which may date from 3,300 BC, a ray of sun penetrates to the back of the burial chamber, but only for a precise moment, on the shortest day of the year.

With its stone alignments, which call to mind an archaic manifestation of writing, with its *geography,* the Earth questions man persistently at Carnac, from a mythic antecedence. An explanation for the white lunar stones, the answer to that riddle, eludes him night and day, challenges him like a dare, almost like a laugh cast before his scant intelligence or his clumsy knowledge, from a time before his time, from before his word — in the opaque language of the earth.

An excessive, almost inquisitorial questioning, a contrast to the emptiness and the calm, to the gray, anonymous neutrality of Brittany's sky stretched uniformly toward the line of the horizon without a cloud, without a streak.

—

In the uneasiness or hermeneutic inadequacy caused by the feeling that one is being questioned, I found myself a few days ago, on a return visit to the megaliths, at the window of an art gallery in the city of Carnac, where my gaze was drawn to a *monumental* painting by Antonio Seguí. The contrast — I realized later — with what I had just seen could not have been more blatant.

As in *The Burial of Count Orgaz,* the canvas is divided horizontally in two unequal parts. But there is an important difference: in Seguí's work the lower or terrestrial register is almost completely empty, filled with nothing but a strange, unsteady, hand-made ladder, like one that might be used for painting walls. The upper or celestial register, on the other hand, seems overpopulated, seems to have been invaded by a restless horde of busy, nervous little men in disparate or disintegrating rows, who appear to be in flight, shaken by tremors, by spasms, Parkinsoned. Although dressed quite neatly and wearing tics, this raucous crowd is attempting to escape from its refuge in the ideal sky, or to break through the edges of the frame at any cost. Are those trembling beings who earned the promised heaven through a precise system of rewards and punishments now disappointed and impatient to leave it, to escape from the apocryphal Paradise? In the heaven they "enjoy" today, the moral recompense of an entire life, does everything continue just as on earth, but forever, with the same disquiet and anxiety but now mechanized and eternal? Is everything a projection of the senses, a Bardo Thödol, an intermediate state before their return to earth? Is God (as represented in the plastic arts) incompetent, vulnerable? Etc.

—

In reality, heaven is empty; in the painting it is questioning and crammed full. Real earth challenges us with a ponderous enigma in millennial stones; the symbolic heaven of the canvas challenges us with another enigma of agitated, modern men.

On the earth in Brittany everything is a mark, a writing in stone, but one we find meaningless; the earth's efforts in the plastic arts afford us nothing but a void, or perhaps the ironic guffaw of a paradox: in fact, there's a Mexican corrido that goes, "For Heaven's climb you'll need to use / a ladder high — a short one too," the second ladder being unnecessary or inadequate for the ascent of the multitudes.

The alignment-covered earth grants no space, no rest to the question that was once an answer: everything is marked by man and acquires the status of a symbol. The symbolic heaven in the painting grants no space either, no physical space: everything is compression and absence of air in its anxious, fleeing mass.

The real and the symbolic oppose each other as in a symmetry, in the Greek sense of that term: two relations, or two pairs that confront and are equal to each other, four terms in equilibrium.

—

An enigma has no solution. The only answer is another enigma. Juxtaposed to the first and lacking any assignable connection, this second enigma belongs to a different field of meaning, which admits of no translation into or possible equivalence with the initial code, the first riddle. Knowledge is not advanced by the attainment of answers, but paradoxically by the addition of new questions, which are always further questions. Next to the undecipherable, one finds another hieroglyphic, another rebus, meant for other eyes. The curious have no choice but to confine themselves to confirming the juxtaposition of the two puzzles. They may even go so far as to attempt a parallel or structural divergence between them, but they will know that the only reason one enigma may be able to elucidate the other is because each has been conceived as a two-part opposition between heaven and earth, and because in both of them the place of the *inscribed* refers, as if this were the essential thing, to the place of things neutral, to *the void*.

T?SEVERO,WHYDOYOUPAINT?SEVERO,WHY
DOYOUPAINT?SEVERO,WHYDOYOUPAINT?SEVE
RO,WHYDOYOUPAINT?SEVERO,WHYDOYOU
PAINT?SEVERO,WHYDOYOUPAINT?SEVERO,WH
YDOYOUPAINT?SEVERO,WHYDOYOUPAINT?SEV
ERO,WHYDOYOUPAINT?SEVERO,WHYDOYOU
PAINT?SEVERO,WHYDOYOUPAINT?SEVERO,WH
YDOYOUPAINT?SEVERO,WHYDOYOUP
VERO,WHYDOYOUPAINT?SEVERO,WHYDOYOUP

SEVERO, WHY DO YOU PAINT?

"Severo, why do you paint?"

"Well, I'll tell you: I paint because I write."

"Is there some relation between the two?"

"For me, they're simply one and the same. The same dog wearing a different collar. Of course the results are different. Although not so different . . . Because painting and writing are like two slopes of a single roof, two sides of a single coin, etc. Maybe it's better to talk in terms of a cube, I mean, there are four faces . . ."

"What do you mean by cube?"

"The cube, in other words, the model for everything, is the drive behind repetition, the obsessive mania to repeat something. I believe that religion is the support of every instance of repetition, that all repetition is prayer. It's common knowledge that

Buddhists relentlessly repeat mantras, those ritual phrases of invocation. Some sects do nothing else: throughout their entire lives they relentlessly repeat mantras. They even repeat the exact same mantra: *Om mani padme hum.* I have always been repetitive. As a child I recited Our Fathers, I think it was because I wanted to scare off the soul of Father Valencia, a saint from my neighborhood. He slept on a board with a brick for a pillow, and was reincarnated as a mangy old turkey buzzard."

"What forms did that repetition take later?"

"Four activities, or four irrepressible drives, all based on the repetition of a gesture. The first one is writing, which involves the repetition of a preparatory ritual — words, rhythms, sometimes whole phrases or paragraphs — as I did in *Maitreya.* The second activity, if you can call it that, is what I have referred to as 'beeromanic prose.' When you drink, you repeat everything, and nothing matters but that repetition. Drunks are repetitive. The third activity is *la drague.* You'll have to forgive me for saying it in French, because I don't know the current term in Spanish. In Cuba they used to say *el flete. Fletear* is to look for casual sexual companionship. This is also a repetition, familiar to everyone without the help of Lacan, because when you find one partner, you look for another, and then another. The fourth activity is painting, in the way I go about it. This involves repeating a single gesture, minute, meticulous, and made with the finest brush there is, the ooooo, which has only about one hair. Always the same, always the same color, more or less, that gesture gradually accumulates on the canvas. It's been estimated that there are thousands in an average work. This 'stitch,' which is what I call each stroke, slowly constructs on its own something that resembles cloth, an ancient weaving, an archaic writing. Some people see cuneiform, others see Hebrew letters, others musical notation, etc. In my recent exhibit people touched the paintings a lot; they thought I had purchased some cloth in India and glued it to the canvas. Other people asked me a terrible question: they wanted to know if I had used a stencil. When I think of the years of work! Each mark, to finish my answer, as I make it, as I write it, is accompanied by the mental recitation of a phrase, a secret phrase, in order to cadence its execution and, I hope, to protect me from something."

"Beyond that explanation, where does this desire to paint come from, where does it originate?"

"Look, it's like your face. Those Chinese features. When I look at you I cannot help thinking of the Buddhas found in the caves of Lo-yang, in China, those gigantic sculptures of dark robust young men possessed of a great serenity.* Nevertheless, if I'm not mistaken, you're pure Spanish . . ."

"——."

"You see, I believe there is some knowledge, something that runs right through us, almost genetically, but it's inexplicable. Before the Conquest, before logic, the men of America wove — in other words, they repeated, and frequently — a single minute gesture in red. This seems to provide an explanation for one of the mysteries of culture: the geoglyphics of Nazca, those giant hummingbirds, masks, and tigers inscribed in the desert. No one knows what they are. People have even gone so far

*The reference here is to the cave temples of Lung-men, near Lo-yang, which were executed or, rather, sculpted in stone according to the wish of the emperor Wei of the North, between 493 and 672. The caves are located alongside a river, all on the west bank, which means they are illuminated by the rising sun.

as to say they are landing strips for extraterrestrials. In one of the most recent theories, they are supports for making very long threads used in weaving, because it took more than seven miles of thread to make some of the shrouds wrapped around those mummies."*

"Everything comes from a great distance."

"After all, my mother is famous for her embroidery."

---

*In *El arte inca y sus orígenes,* Henri Stierlin, author of the hypothesis I have summarized here, also studies and explicates the art and craftsmanship of the Paracas-Nazca area: four millennia of evolution best exemplified by textiles, the mantles of Paracas-Necropolis, for example. The same author speaks of obsessive motifs, which in this case are stylized felines. The textiles formed part of what were referred to as "bundles" of the dead; they were tapestry-woven and decorated with embroidery. The warp is made of cotton, the weft of wool. These works date from 300 – 100 AD. Some can be found in the Museo Arqueológico in Lima. The Great Hummingbird, one of the geoglyphics from the Nazca-Palpa region, is 95 meters tall and was drawn without a break, inscribed in the desert in a single line. The dryness of the climate has preserved these relics for more than 1,500 years, at the edge of a fertile plain.

Because It's Real

CHRIST'SASCENTANIMAGEOFCHRIST'SASCENT
ANIMAGEOFCHRIST'SASCENTANIMAGEOFCHRI
ST'SASCENTANIMAGEOFCHRIST'SASCENTANIM
AGEOFCHRIST'SASCENTANIMAGEOFCHRIST'SA
SCENTANIMAGEOFCHRIST'SASCENTANIMAGEO
FCHRIST'SASCENTANIMAGEOFCHRIST'SASCEN
TANIMAGEOFCHRIST'SASCENTANIMAGEOFCHRI
ST'SASCENTANIMAGEOFCHRIST'SASCENTANI
MAGEOFCHRIST'SASCENTANIMAGEOFCHRIST'S

AN IMAGE OF CHRIST'S ASCENT

On the tiny tomb of the canon Aymeric, from the late thirteenth century, in the museum of the Augustinians in Toulouse, the soul of the deceased appears as a little wooden or clay figure with movable joints, or as an asexual and anonymous child emerging with great difficulty from the rigid dignitary, after the cowl of the canonical almuce has been folded back.

The medieval soul is almost always a stiff whitish little dwarf expelled from the mouth of the expiring like a belch or vomit. It remains suspended, flying with open arms over the head of the deceased: a bloodless, weightless fetish, or a well-developed fetus waiting for an opportune angel to raise him to the feet of Christ.

On the tomb of a bishop from Tarragona, however, the migration of the soul is represented as a miniaturized — even mitered — double of the dying man. Kneeling and praying in the midst of a shroud held at the corners by four angels — as if they were going to make a dummy leap — he ascends slowly into the arms of the Redeemer.

On the tomb executed by Andrea Bregno in Santa Maria sopra Minerva in Rome for Cardinal Giovanni Diego de Coca, who died in 1477, the soul, painted this time on the back wall, appears as a subtle emanation sprouting from the head of the marble recumbent. No angel takes away or holds the soul as it ascends. A kindly Christ with a little beard simply picks it up at the moment it departs.

Throughout his life Philippe Ariès catalogued this moving and even naive iconography of the last moment.

—

Under an avalanche in a secure camping tent, nourishing themselves with nothing but suntan lotion and snow, two French mountain climbers survived burial for three weeks.

Back from this near death, when questioned on

television about the "experience" the couple had
lived through, their testimony in no way differed —
if we forget the differences between the codes of
sculpted stone, oil paint, and words — from the epitaphs on the tombs described above.

Over their numb, stiff, and soon almost frozen
bodies, they saw rise something like a double, or like
a weightless image of the body itself, which was
relieved by the expulsion of that simulacrum and
detached already from pain and hunger.

Calm and rested, she said, they floated serenely
over that residue at the center of a neutral space
from which they could either ascend — she doesn't
know to where — or return to their pitiful appear-
ances, to their emptied "continents."

They decided to animate those continents again,
despite intolerable muscle spasms and the foul smell
that, according to the man, emanated from "the
body addressing itself."

Our iconography of life, as everyone knows, is
vast, prolific, and colorful. Death, or the Ascent, is
exhausted, as you can see, in a single image.

Writing is useless. It does nothing to rescue those who are swept away by a sea of lava, who lie already beneath that stone.

Writing, and the rest. A lesson in the ephemeral for anyone who looks helplessly at those bodies covered with mud, shielded, asphyxiated by a scab that slowly hardens, marble-white hair, blood-drained faces. Vomited by the earth, the water, black with coal and ash, rises until it suffocates the pale praying mouth, their sex organs ripped off with one stroke.

In the face of these passing images, a healthy divertissement is the diligent threading of words, aligning them precisely and rhythmically: absurd hobby of the idle, benign vice of the unemployed.

Blink your eyes, string a phrase together, and an entire city has been buried, every sleeping citizen petrified, the children hugging their toys, their dogs: porous statues of lava.

Writing presumes a lack of awareness, or slight irresponsibility, on the part of the one who forgets or evades while, caught in the magma, the precipitous shroud solidifying around her, a little girl asks her mother to pray.

SOLDIERS

They pillage, sack, burn, annihilate everything in their path, these little lead soldiers. They know not why they do it, nor in the name of what law. They arrive frightened and guilty; after a few months they are efficient killing machines.

Scrofulous and naked, they found themselves in a sandy courtyard beside a stone well in the shade of eaves where — the desert wind may have been blowing — they were ambushed by the Afghan resistance.

They then told how they had razed a hovel and machine-gunned its seventeen inhabitants — sure targets huddled together inside. The first of the soldiers, who kicked the door open, paid for it by scattering his own guts on the floor. The others threw grenades in the windows and incinerated the whole family. The smell of scorched bodies, burning blood, excrement, and urine was so strong that the soldiers, after that brave assault, fainted or doubled over with spasms of vomit. But they continued to liberate their sister country.

(They're given heroin and opium, so that it will all seem like a game.)

THE STREET CLEANER OF MEXICO CITY

On the nineteenth of September, at 7:20 A.M., the earth trembled in Mexico.

Three states, with their millennial remains and blueprints for the future, were annihilated; a third of the capital also collapsed.

In the heart of the city, at dawn, a sleepy but scrupulous cleaner was fulfilling his duties, listlessly pushing his broom like an obedient robot and making perfect lines on a patio of reddish stones, a twenty-four-hour parking lot, or simply some empty ground hemmed in by recent skyscrapers.

Upon hearing the sound of the quake, gripped by a more than human panic — animals sense it before a cataclysm; chickens try to fly to the tree tops, dogs tremble — the street cleaner threw down his broom and fled in terror through the giant blocks of reinforced concrete, cables, screeching metal, burning furniture, bricks, and mangled human bodies plunging on either side of the straight line he followed in his flight, one that seemed to have been traced to save him, by the same hand that ordained the disaster, as unthinking and light as the hand of a child destroying a cardboard model for the fun of it.

Once far away, when his legs failed him — buckled with fear — and he was out of breath, he turned around, alone in the midst of the landslide and in the palpable silence that followed, and stood stiffly like a jade priest, contemplating the extent of the disaster.

He remained motionless for a few minutes. He doesn't know what he thought or said to himself.

What he does know for certain is that then he took the road back, through pyramids of irreversible ruins that resembled ancient tumuli and mausoleums.

And he continued to sweep.

—

The international press — viz. *Le Monde* that same day — together with the brief chronicle of the apocalypse, portrays the frenzied course of the street cleaner and his inane gesture or insolent indifference as one more example of popular madness: the loss of an already precarious consciousness in the face of an irreparable destruction of such magnitude.

What we should see, however, in the street cleaner's delirious gesture and his swaggering gratitude in the face of the absurd is precisely a desire to efface absurdity. We should see the trace of a violent, perhaps inborn wisdom: Ignore the gods' atrocious diversion as a way of deflating them; don't listen to the sounds of their bloodthirsty crap games.

—

Those forgettable broomstrokes will remain after the chaos, as long as someone remembers them, as the best definition of Man — as his rebellion against the gratuitous behavior of the lesser gods who labored over our universe, and against cosmic disorder — as the best proof of his reason.

On an Autumn Night,
I Think of My Friends

Years ago, in Tibet — or in the symbolic region that stretches from those overlapping patches of ochre earth north of India to the first excessive statues of Mao — I bought a vast blank book that I covered with silky and garish gilded paper. The book was inscribed by a draftsman with an intricate purple-and-orange iconography whose ultimate referent, I suppose, is Buddhism. The pages — and this is a less frequent detail in those miniature Himalayan realms — are marked with the letters of our alphabet.

Remembering the words of a friend who regretted more the confiscation of his address book than he did his taciturn days spent in prison, I decided to compose in the thick volume a directory of names and addresses that would be as meticulous and up-to-date as was required by my phobia, my lack of close ties: the phantom that haunts every exile.

Sometime later — I had a taste then for the sudden mirrorings between East and West — the writer Hector Murena called me at my hotel in Buenos Aires to announce, amid *vamos, che* and other idiomatic devices to soften his harsh news, the death of Calvert Casey.

Some hours later, at the house of María Rosa Oliver, who had known and admired him since Havana days, we roused ourselves from an embarrassing funereal silence by doing something that, deep down, shocked me, because we Cubans adhere so strictly to our mournful rituals: "Let's drink to Calvert's memory."

From the Tibetan book I never dared to erase his name.

Striking out the address of a friend because of that absence we insist upon thinking is temporary, substituting another for him, or marking him with a sign that indicates the definitive uselessness of his address — a cross would be the most brutal and grotesque — or erasing to leave an empty line, indicating a lack between the aligned and identical letters, would be like eradicating him all over again, as if I were an accomplice of the void, subjecting him to another death within death, excluding him from the ink's blue day, from the sketchiest and most denotative writing: a true disappearance for one who has lived by disseminating words.

Many others — so many that with them death has only confirmed the pulse of its repetition — have come, letter by letter, to indicate their fictitious presence, the empty simulacrum of their identity in what is already another *Tibetan Book of the Dead.*

The beginning letters of the alphabet, either through my Latin affiliations or the Reaper's dark anagrammatic mania, are the most solicited. One of the most luxuriant — several addresses, rural or secret telephone numbers — B, was decimated with one blow: Barthes.

Intact each year and increasingly ineffectual by definition, the Book has been gradually approaching another genre, both unexpected and generous: the novel, or biographical fiction. Its reading invents for the disappeared an anecdotal life on paper — freer or more apocryphal the more time passes: through error or oblivion, scenes and chapters which they perhaps never lived become accentuated and, thanks to my archival perseverance, sustain them in another life of myths and characters. Meticulously parallel to each day I consume this life, barely less deceptive than supposed reality, by using, writing, or phoning the addresses and numbers that are still valid.

Thus I see Calvert, though I don't know if he ever was, sitting at the bar in the Tencén — phonetic adaptation of *ten cent* from the populous empire to the north — in Havana, with Lezama (the liaison is improbable) or with Virgilio (the coincidence is a sure bet) shredding to pieces layers of Bakelite, crystal, aluminum, and copper, all the solids and liquids of the establishment, to return them to their births in the remote geological formation of the island, in a hyperbolic and flagrant flashback. Virgilio, as usual, confronts a lethargic waitress with one of his metaphysical aporias, a Cuban koan, by demanding a papaya milkshake, but, because of his deficient liver, one made without first sugar, then milk, any kind of malt, crushed ice, and above all — to top off his vesicular phobia — without papaya.

Calvert appears again — this reference is precise — in my house at Sceaux. We are on the balcony, a grayish and brief summer in the suburbs. He speaks to me of India. I know that he's one of the first to do so with the identifiable passion I now know so well and share, which contradicts the precedence of the Tibetan book and also — but here I shuffle the dates — of a postcard from India I receive from Rome, torn out of carelessness, stuck together again, and accompanied by an explanatory letter: "The unconscious is well aware of these faux pas."

Another memory of the same day, and of his — always laborious — manner of speaking: he evokes the recent death of his mother and adds, with repeated though involuntary and, as I realized later, revealing vacillations: "We were so different . . ."

He liked the place where I live, with its calm atmosphere of a park in the provinces and the nearby Romanesque-looking church where fin de siècle busts of troubadours form an enthusiastic and dark-green *ronde* around their instructor in prosody, Frédéric Mistral.

The news from Rome: in a letter he contradicts or reproaches me — as Lezama did when I suggested a similarity between *Paradiso* and Gadda's work — for the influence of Virgilio Piñera I perceive in his recent narratives: keys of a piano which don't jump back when pushed down by the fingers, signs of soggy abandonment, misery, or ennui. An aura at once dense and icy, orthogonal and stagy gestures, and the ferocious and Kafkaesque profile of players in Piñera's version of Gombrowicz take over the decrepit sets, the sullen stained rooms.

The latest news from Rome: a mutual friend withdraws Calvert's remains from the vault to place them in the family shrine. Upon leaving the cemetery — she writes me — she's caught by a tree branch that detains her affectionately, gratefully.

Final note: the names cited in these pages, almost randomly, belong to those I have not erased from the *Tibetan Book of the Dead*. I remember them today with a dedication written by one of them: *Le soir, en automne, je pense à mes amis:* Calvert Casey, Hector Murena, María Rosa Oliver, Roland Barthes, José Lezama Lima, Virgilio Piñera, Witold Gombrowicz.

—

Addenda, June 1986, to the final note: Italo Calvino, Emir Rodríguez Monegal, José Bianco.

BYJESSEPORTRAITSBYJESSEPORTRAITSBYJE
SSEPORTRAITSBYJESSEPORTRAITSBYJESSEP
ORTRAITSBYJESSEPORTRAITSBYJESSEPORTR
AITSBYJESSEPORTRAITSBYJESSEPORTRAITSB
YJESSEPORTRAITSBYJESSEPORTRAITSBYJES
SEPORTRAITSBYJESSEPORTRAITSBYJESSEPO
RTRAITSBYJESSEPORTRAITSBYJESSEPORTRAI
TSBYJESSEPORTRAITSBYJESSEPORTRAITSBY
JESSEPORTRAITSBYJESSEPORTRAITSBYJESS

PORTRAITS BY JESSE

The better-off natives used to go to the photographer's too, just once in their lives, when they saw death was near. Their photos were large, all the same size, hung in handsome gilt frames near the altars to their ancestors. All these photographs of different people, and I've seen many of them, gave practically identical results, the resemblance was stunning. It wasn't because all old people look alike, but because the portraits themselves were invariably touched up in such a way that any facial peculiarities, if there were any left, were minimized. All the faces were prepared in the same way to confront eternity, all toned down, all uniformly rejuvenated.

— Marguerite Duras, *The Lover*

If I begin with this long quotation from Marguerite Duras's recent novel in order to speak about a new book and a current exhibition, Jesse A. Fernández's

107

*Portraits,** it is from the pleasure of creating a kind of antiphrasis, of revealing the *negative*. The art of Jesse Fernández is the exact opposite, the parody, and the contradiction of those icons for the altars to the ancestors that Duras discovered in Saigon in the 1940s, but which could be in any suburban shopwindow, in faded colors, beside the stiff wedding poses, the "sweet sixteen" celebration, or the healthy euphoria of a christening.

Jesse portrays the opposite, but also the irony of that idealization. What drives his industrious hand, his apparently neutral gaze, and the focusing of his objective — I know: there is no word more deceptive than *objective* applied to the art of photography — is the reverse of what drives him to retouch preposthumous portraits to the point of anonymity, giving them a finish which, by virtue of denying it, produces a mortuary effect. No: Jesse immerses himself in the individual, identifying to such a degree that nothing external to the subject defines that individual — not even an attitude or a gesture that might prove "revealing" because of some anecdotal detail

Portraits by Jesse Fernández, ICI, Madrid, 1984. Exhibition at the Museo Español de Arte Contemporáneo.

and thus come to signify a personality captured in the moment, in flight, as if that attitude or that gesture had been stolen from the subject's conscious image or composure.

We are inevitably reminded of the portraits from the Roman Republic and, even more, of Etruscan funerary busts. It was necessary then to present oneself to death without the slightest "finish" — on the contrary, with a persistent individual panoply: baldness, warts, the stigmata of age: these are the true signs of identity.

In order to provide the individual with that graphic document in view of his "passing" or his posterity, Jesse retains only the face, and of the face, despite the proliferation of its details and the natural excess of its signs, only one thing: the gaze. These portraits look, look at us, from the depths of an identity. Or from an exile. Or from a sadness often unknown to the subject himself, and which a particular silence, an echo chamber — which Jesse creates around him, at a given moment — amplifies and reveals.

The signifying detail, what Roland Barthes in his book *Camera Lucida* called the *punctum,* has been eliminated here, or rather, dissolved in the vast geography of the face, in that *substance* which from the depths of time, from solitude, or simply from genetics gazes at us, interrogates us, and includes us in its space.

To create his echo-chamber effect, that is, to leave the subject alone with his gaze and objectivize it in an almost tactile way, Jesse employs only a minimal staging — or setting. A small ritual that proceeds, contrary to the ornate trappings of other photographers, by means of elimination or asepsis.

When I review a book or a painting, besides the limitations of the critical result, I'm always left with a frustration: I have not witnessed the execution of the work, I don't know how the artist conceived or structured the object I envelop in my language. For the first time, the opposite occurred: I witnessed the execution of one of these photographs, the construction of one of these portraits, since I was one of the subjects; I saw the echo chamber come into being.

As soon as I found out that Jesse Fernández was going to photograph me, I began to drink mineral water; I put on my best suit and some discreet make-up. I composed for myself a more or less seductive character and immediately tried to take him — Jesse — to the Flore, the Parisian café I've been frequenting for a quarter of a century and where I pictured myself surrounded by acquaintances, in a favorable, almost protective "light."

In an effort to produce the most flattering image, I suggested various places, "poses," and arrangements; Jesse dissuaded me with Socratic ability, using arguments about angles, or "chiaroscuros." "There are too many reflections," he replied, almost sadly, about the Flore.

We ended up beside a peeling wall and a discreet café table. I futilely arranged my tie. I looked at the camera. A silence. Nothing happened.

Only a long time later, when I discovered not my portrait but the ensemble of his portraits, a gallery extending over almost thirty years of work and over all the continents and styles of being in this century, did I understand that Jesse had shown me, with his successive renunciations and eliminations, what occurs in vain every day, as if before a blind man, in the mirror, or in the iris of another's eye: the substance of a gaze.

ATEIGHTINTHEFLOREATEIGHTINTHEFLOREATEI
GHTINTHEFLOREATEIGHTINTHEFLOREATEIGHTI
NTHEFLOREATEIGHTINTHEFLOREATEIGHTINTH
EFLOREATEIGHTINTHEFLOREATEIGHTINTHEFL
OREATEIGHTINTHEFLOREATEIGHTINTHEFLORE
ATEIGHTINTHEFLOREATEIGHTINTHEFLOREATEI
GHTINTHEFLOREATEIGHTINTHEFLOREATEIGHT-
INTHEFLOR   IGHTINT
HEFLOREATEIGHTINTHEFLOREATEIGHTINTHEF

AT EIGHT IN THE FLORE

"At eight in the Flore": thus we would end our brief telephone conversations, among other things because Roland Barthes — even though he had dreamed of having three different telephones — hated the abrupt intrusion of the phone upon his private life.

Then, at eight o'clock sharp and always at the same table, a meticulous ritual would begin, regulated like a chess game, one whose precision I now realize was significant.

Roland loved coffee almost to an excess, but hated alcohol.

Or he identified with the *non-mixed* — to make use of Michelet's legendary classification, always useful for justifying all culinary loyalties and antipathies — the coffee at the Flore certainly is strong, undiluted, and decidedly "Italian" — and he hated the *mixed*.

112

Now, alcohol, at least as it is conceived by my diligence, is *mixed,* par excellence. And to an excess, almost a braggart's fanfare of *mixed:* the Bloody Mary achieves its fire by obeying the rhetorical precepts of the Baroque age: the sudden juxtaposition of opposites.

A Caravaggesque drink, the Bloody Mary quells the vodka's tartar violence with the velvety affection of the tomato, and its zany pepper with the jolt of its icy frappé. The mannered touch of a cherry — something like a ruby in the right ear of a Bronzino — attenuates the Mexican tabasco, sharp and sacrificial like curare. This blasphemy, the awkward addition of the fruit, is spreading increasingly throughout the world. There are those who have reached the savagery of sprinkling the edge of the glass with a snowfall of sugar.

But back to the Flore. The Barthesian rejection of the *mixed,* which I consumed daily with a vengeance, was aggravated — like a rhetorical figure gone wrong because of an excessive adverb — by two habits of mine that accompanied my drinking and provoked his greatest disapproval.

First, I always wanted to taste his coffee, an irritating whim if you keep in mind the minute portions of coffee — no doubt because of the concentration characteristic of everything *non-mixed* — served at the Flore. Secondly, what was even worse was the indirect way I would request the abovementioned sip, imitating paternal Cuban mannerisms with gross circumlocutions like "Give me what the doctor prescribes," or with a mere gesture, now an obvious sign by dint of repetition.

That opposition was only the first, followed invariably by the most theatrical or tense moment of all: deciding upon a restaurant, this time a dichotomy we shared.

Like the *iron-wood* Wittgenstein discusses, which signifies an empty "cluster," our restaurant was an impossibility if we stood by the very terms of its definition. Above all it had to be quiet — this silence excluded, above all, Russian music — but at the same time animated, full of life, even euphoric; the waiters had to be pleasant, gratifying — the term we used then — but not too friendly or "enterprising." Finally, it had to be a place where Roland was not recognized, praised or punished by that flattery which without exception proved to him that he had written or said exactly the opposite of what he intended; of course we also had to avoid an intolerable anonymity. (Then the opposition would start up again: for R.B., as far as the dishes were concerned, *non-mixed* was obligatory — if possible, home cooking or even country-style dishes. I, on the other hand, would try to recover the lost prestige of Cuban cuisine with an excessive assortment of "trimmings" and sauces.)

Our evening together would generate a whole system of identifications and rejections, of small antipathies and discreet delights. A system that functioned upon a rigorously contradictory and binary basis; in other words, a *structural* system.

—

The reading, at once distant and intimate, of Roland Barthes that I could do today — relating to him as I believe he wanted, that is, as a detached accomplice — would be no more than an extension of those "pairs of opposites," transposing in a more ample space the terms of our simple contradiction: a whole ideology of Barthesian taste, or if you prefer, a whole *bathmology,* that science of the degrees or strata of values themselves, which Roland wanted to found; a knowledge that, like an axiology, would have made it immediately possible to assign anything, or any discourse, its exact place on a scale.

Let us extend then, in this hypothetical bathmology, the simpleminded opposition to the Bloody Mary. Whoever doesn't like this drink, an example of the *mixed* par excellence, will have to reject Maria Callas — a blend of theatricality, vocal art, and myth — Miró's paintings, politico-sexual discourse, Erik Satie's music. The same individual will like cinnamon, fresh cheese, the smell of newly cut grass, of toast in the morning, the clear voice of Panzera, a tenor from the turn of the century who rejected all breathless expressivity and all theatricality, a pure vocal denotation.

But beyond the anecdotal, what would be the true support of this science, its final sense? What logic sustains and animates, at times violently, the science of stages that link together and open out until they define the limits of a space — as if they were weaving it — a space that belongs only to them, to their kindred, and radically excludes the Other, deaf echo of otherness, trace of the antipodal lover?

The final and central meaning, the absent knot

of these networks of opposites that proliferate by annexing similarities, similar situations and things, is none other than pleasure. That little theater of accessories exposed suddenly to the stage lights or rejected, of characters coveted or undesirable, of trivialities that immediately turn into objects of adoration or a barely dissembled scorn, hides, behind a meticulous representation and its impeccable operation, a *marked object*, the object of absolute desire or of total repulsion.

From the very first contradiction, everything, even when pretending the opposite, does nothing but name, invoke, avoid this object.

Unless that whole game of contradictions does not conceal an even stronger desire, a doubly marked object: binarity itself, which for Barthes — he admits this in his *Barthes par lui-même* — was a true object of love.

The marked object, emerging always on the horizon and nevertheless invisible and nocturnal, watched over Roland Barthes at every disjunction, at every word, in every sentence.

A curious analogy: a diverging or forking ideogram constitutes the basis of his painting, shaped as a vacillation between two strokes, or between two Japanese pencils with different felts, or between two identically blue inks.

The same ideogram governs the always hand-written corrections of his texts, forming not an arborescence, as in Proust's pages, but rather a binary labyrinth, which always has two entries or exits, the two dry branches of a cherry tree.

The marked object, then, is what awaits us in the void *between the two branches,* and not what we find at their tips.

Waiting in calm detachment. Waiting at eight in the Flore.

I dreamt that I was sleeping with Italo Calvino. We were dressed severely in suits and ties, under the same wrinkly, dull-white, rectangular sheet, just ironed: in it visible folds, or orthogonal shadows of another white, etched neat, even squares that glittered in the beige or yellowish glare of the night, as if glowing with a different light — pus-colored or waxen, pale and sickly.

We were dazed by the density of the saturated, humid air, a uniform birdless gray over the light-green lawn and the pine trees. Perhaps it wasn't drowsiness or the assiduous sluggishness of a tropical siesta or a postprandial languor that devoured us but, rather, some other lethargy, a blinder absence: a spiraling blackout of thought, a senile corrosion of time, a simulated death, or a drunken stupor.

We spoke of our native country. Familiar green: the region of Pinar del Río, with its bottles full of fireflies and the Lezamesque arch in the valleys of Viñales. The insistent sweet smell of our childhood: tobacco leaves fold like caterpillars, knotty symmetrical nerves, at the touch of black hands.

Our rigid and circumspect fathers, in their guayaberas and wide-brimmed hats, recently dismounted from their horses, posed before thatched huts, between two royal palms, as if for a Sunday portrait by Abela or the painter Victor Manuel.

What was the writer saying to me, in an identifiable and familiar tone, that got lost in his accent? From what evening or buried memory were we protecting ourselves, what useless refuge were we toasting? Some cheap, recurrent background music studded with Mexican sayings, or that rasping, sluggish diction close to Calvert's, blurred his words. I knew that they were meant for me, that it was for me he had rescued them from vigil or from yesterday's text. They did not form, however, any recognizable or daily discourse, any advice or premonition. Or perhaps there were no words, or they were not articulated, individual and real, outlined and clear-edged.

No silence scanned and penetrated them, making them intelligible and meaningful. Or else it was a foggy language, blurred ideograms that abstracted, reduced the expressions of his face to their purest form: the upper lip slightly protruding, the brow creased, the eyelids wrinkled and tight-shut, the iris of an Assyrian hunter.

A woven, button-tipped pyramidal cap of thick wool protected my austere partner from the astral cold: on the island the magnetic, watery light of the moon invoked bronchial quakes and asthmatic seizures.

Hieroglyphics, vast gestural marks were everywhere. As in an inverted riddle, or a gibberish of gestures, the slow, indecipherable movements of the other sleeper suggested to me a behavior at once spontaneous and urgent, some simple and inevitable "directions for use" designated with pointing hands, numbered arrows, and dotted lines.

With the open palm of his right hand, or with the tip of his fingers, he gently tapped the sheet on his side, as if to call a trained and obedient animal, a Tibetan dog with a flattened nose and a black tongue. Or perhaps he was inviting me with that gesture to sink further down into our common bed, as if to listen to an incredible yet logical story, or to a soporific reading. Or to lay my head on his chest. Or to go back to sleep.

—

Death, then, was this: a closeness at once familiar and futile, the affectionate proximity of the incomprehensible. A different lethargy: not the euphoric sleepwalking of alcohol, inhabited by images and heavings, nor the definitive penalty of barbiturates, nor the instantaneous absence of orgasm, nor the void, nor oblivion, but instead the discreet seduction of nonbeing, the bland magnetism of the unformulated and nonmanifest, as if the body were yielding to a facile or lazy state. Or letting itself go, at once fascinated and sluggish, toward a repose that grew deeper and more radical, eclipsed by an insipid whiteness, a gratuitous stupor.

The sudden abyss of the satori, Santa Teresa's nothingness, the clear negativity of the Canticle, the silence of Sakyamuni under the tree now appeared as lucid lapses, with pure edges at once taut and transparent. Death, on the other hand, seemed an

incessant word, a fallacious and irresponsible bab-
ble, an intermediate stage generated by our own pet-
tiness: a faded silent film, the projection of an
impoverished consciousness, an inane ephemeral
fiction.

I cannot pay homage to Emir Rodríguez Monegal — especially not a posthumous homage, where one tends to lionize, almost always fatuously — without asking myself at the same time, as if seeking a realistic effect: What is writing, and why or for whom do I write?

Because, you see, Emir was very close not only to my writing — for which, in part, I am indebted to him — but also to its deepest motivations, its justification, and its ultimate meaning.

Approaching my fiftieth year, and with over a quarter of a century of texts wrought by melancholy and exile, I still believe that writing has no immediate use, that the repercussions or impalpable echoes a book produces are lost in a diffuse distance, or in the memory of an absent reader we will never find, or in vague commentaries or the criticism of our persistent detractors. I do believe, however, that writing emanates from a given moment and is for a given interlocutor who justifies that ephemeral moment, prolonging or amplifying a casual conversation under an enormous clock in the Parisian quarter of Saint-Lazare, projecting it upon a limitless night, an ink-dark night.

This was my conversation, under that clock, at the office of *Mundo Nuevo* with Emir Rodríguez Monegal. My other mentor from those times, in which I now see myself unreal and blurry as in an old film, was Roland Barthes, but his assent or suggestions were very different: he either did or didn't approve, praise, or quote me in his books, but he never participated in the birth, never urged me to write. In my long years at *Mundo Nuevo,* and in the complicity that followed that polemical adventure, I learned that a writer produces only upon request, or as the Argentines say, by the job.

Nothing is more immobilizing or less encouraging than those letters in which we are asked to contribute "something about something" for an incipient journal, without specifications, limitations, or deadlines. Emir's persuasion was exactly the opposite: his request was precise, centered — as one aims at a target — upon a given object, designed to form part of a whole, to elucidate something. Or to strike against something. Never — except in the now mythic times of the magazine *Ciclón,* in Cuba — had I known such an effective provocation to write, such a generous listener, before Emir. Or after.

All attentive listening ultimately implies a discussion, a criticism. Or, better, a criticism of Criticism. Emir listened above all to his own desire to write as well as to the texts preceding it, the commentaries on the authors he was going to *read,* in the most semiological sense of the term, as one deciphers a hieroglyph or the opaque, labyrinthine narrative of a dream. He listened to those texts — their exegesis acknowledged, accepted — not to confirm them in his own writing but, on the contrary, to discuss, to submit them to the violent light of paradox and contradiction. Thus, in his last and penetrating works on Lautréamont, Emir Rodríguez Monegal examines the very basis of his countryman's metaphors and syntactical distortions, and discovers, where traditional criticism has seen only subjectivity or even delirium, an anchor in reality, a recognizable foundation. He discovers in Lautréamont's Montevidean childhood and its natural violence, which others attributed to the excesses of Biblical readings, and in Hermosilla's *Rhetoric* the evident models that would serve the syntactical deconstruction undertaken in the *Chants de Maldoror.* Emir Rodríguez Monegal's work is critical, then, against criticism, against the mainstream, against common — that is, ordinary — sense.

The most essential remains to be said: prevailing friendship, constant affection, the letter or the postcard intersecting with words of encouragement, projects, itineraries, drawings, photographs.

In order to give the deceased a status of transcendence and purity, the Greeks, in their funerary steles, portrayed him naked and smiling, surrounded by his favorite objects and his faithful dogs. Without hysteria or drama he extends a hand to his entourage, or to his best friend.

This is how I would portray Emir's parting, as a pledge of fidelity, or a congratulatory salute for the clarity achieved in the eternal life, which is the life of texts. As a promise and a greeting.

21 JULY 1969

Sr. Severo Sarduy
In Paris

Dear friend:

I have received your words which summon me to
the feast of the baroque pineapple of Sceaux, pictured in your lovely illustration. Every trip is highly
problematic for me, however; since I did not acquire
the habit of traveling in my youth, now that I've
reached maturity, every translocation takes on a hysterical pace characterized by banal worries, manias,
and annoyances. At this point hopping about holds
little attraction for me, and in truth what I would
like to do is spend a year in Paris or Madrid, resting
and recuperating, because in recent years my health,

128

although not precarious, has been unstable. If I could make the trip with my wife, I think everything would move along at a nice andantino pace. Everything strikes me as confusion, as clouds galloping, but then the ray of grace begins its work, and the day eventually takes shape. You, no doubt, will understand my moods quite well.

Back to our dear bits of flesh. You ask my opinion about whether the book should appear in one volume or two. It would not displease me if both *were to appear in bookstores at the same moment,* although I would prefer a single volume, because if a space of time, however brief, were to intervene between the first volume and the second, the unity of the work would suffer from that delay. Any interval would open a lacuna in the center of the work. I also realize that the publisher's reasons for issuing the work in either one volume or two must have a sound basis. You have shown such affectionate support for *Paradiso* all along — and this has afforded me much happiness — and you will know how to find the right leverage, the best solution.

I'm already enamoored of the volume of Baudelaire's collected works that you people are about to publish. I await this gift, which all by itself will occasion an Easter or a christening. One of Baudelaire's most significant assertions is like a prism, and I turn it often: "What makes the world revolve is nothing but universal misunderstanding; through misunderstanding the whole world reaches agreement. Because, unfortunately, if everyone were to understand each other, no one would ever get along."

How true of our own times: if it weren't for alienation, contemporary life could not achieve its logos. If alienation were to be suppressed, life would become a plain of snow, in the same way that Saint Augustine called early for the existence of heretics and, much later, Gracián accepted with tolerant bitterness that "this world creates harmony from disharmony." That's why Baudelaire had to seek help from the devil of lucidity, a kind of alienation.

Affectionately,

J. Lezama Lima

NOTES TO THE LETTER

"The baroque pineapple of Sceaux" is more the product of local confectionery than a Lezamesque metaphor for my letter of invitation: Seuil, where *Paradiso* was being published in the series that I currently inspire, had invited Lezama to Paris to celebrate the appearance of the book. In the still life formed by Lezama's writing, carefully perfected and asymmetrical like a Spanish still life — although in it the delicacies and fruits of the Peninsula have been replaced by Cuba's sizzling cornucopia, and okra, *caimitos*, guavas, and mangoes blur the precise, attenuated geometry of apples — what prevails is a "glazed" or candied nature. Syrup, that artless alchemy of the nation's sugar, provides a perfect finish and frosts everything, packing fruits and pastries into a saccharine layer of topping, which in the heat and over time becomes cloudy and thickens like heavy glass. This cloying quality, however, is nothing but the stamp of a vaster conquest or appropriation, in which Lezama acknowledges the spirit of Cuba's Mambí patriots, the signs of their insurrection, an inkling of subversion: ". . . the arrogance

of Spanish cuisine as well as the sensuality and sur-
prises of Cuban cuisine, which may seem Spanish
but declared its independence in 1868."[1]

I am not forgetting the actual iced fruits in question, bursting with their own unadulterated juices in
barely thickened fillings and adorned with their own
crowns; along with the small, still bloody trophies
from forest hunts, they brighten the streets of
Sceaux and renew in some way the festive baroque
tradition of the Castle, which Colbert entrusted to
Claude Perrault, and which Le Brun, with the help
of Coysevox and Girardon, would temper with his
blazing chariots of Dawn and ceiling decorations
insistent in their monarchical metaphors. Racine's
Phaedre, to which Lezama refers constantly, was
performed at the inauguration; later, for a visit of
the sovereign and Madame de Maintenon, the court
poet composed an "Idyll of Sceaux," a celebration
devoted to the victories of the Sun King.

The banquet I attempted to offer the master[2]
was enameled, then, by both the gastronomical mar-
vels from areas around Paris and the textual connotations of a time — the classicism of metrical rigor,
the baroque of the Racinian image — that in Lezama

achieved the category of *era,* those periods of men's imagination when great poetry is lived plentifully.[3]

—

"Since I did not acquire the habit of traveling in my youth." Lezama's life is marked by something that was also the center of his poetic system and the title of his key work: *La fijeza* [fixedness]. What is more, confinement, a persistent immobility, a phobia of all displacement: "Every translocation takes on a hysterical pace." The "everything" that strikes him "as confusion, as clouds galloping" is the strident set from an opera, or the possibility of moving, the *potens* — to use his term — of the drift, as if the body were *fixed* by genetically inflexible tethers to a familiar city, a circle halfway between the legendary house of the mother and the "unmentionable fiesta" of the island where he was born.

Lezama's biographers make no mention of trips. Armando Álvarez Bravo points out, however, a short stay in Mexico when Lezama, in contact "with the mainland, with the American landscape, enlarged his ideas about this cosmos, of which he knew only one aspect, the islands." Then in 1950 he "takes another, short trip, this time to Jamaica. Basing himself on this trip and on his previous journey, he begins to forge a theory about 'American expression.'"[4] I think that from then on — unless Eloísa Lezama Lima has another version of this — the intimidating area, the region hostile to all displacement narrows gradually, reducing the safeguarded territory that the Mother buoys as she goes about her daily tasks, marking it with her care, as if Lezama's respiratory difficulties prevented him from moving too far from the cadence of that other breath, from an ideal rhythm of contact with space and air, guarantee of both survival and serenity.

In poems like *El arco invisible de Viñales* [The invisible arch of Viñales] he left proof of his travels by interrupting the pure phonetic enjoyment occasioned by his poetry with details so realistic and minute that they eventually form something like a narrative — the boy selling stalactites, the bottle full of fireflies where he saves the ten céntimos he earns for each stone and which he places under his pillow; his brother, a Picassoist juggler; his mother fanning the door to shoo away a lizard; his sister tiptoeing by so as not to wake anyone, sneaking off to meet her soldier: a vignette that portrays the Cuban peasant family in a way reminiscent of the vignettes of Abela or Victor Manuel. Lezama was not even an island traveler — like those in my own family — addicted to train number 1, which covered Cuba's six provinces at laughable or outlandish speeds, making local stops that filled the platforms to overflowing.

It's true that he went frequently to Bauta, near Havana, the parish of Angel Gaztelu, a priest who was a member of the editorial board of *Orígenes,*[5] to attend Sunday banquets that were Creole anthologies of after-dinner conversations marked by siesta-time sonnets, and also to the weddings and christenings of his friends, faithful, like the rhythm of the seasons, to the cyclic return of Christian commemorations and rituals.[6]

Nevertheless, the sensuality of knowing, the huge number of similitudes, connections, and references this immobile man threads together is so great that as early as the 1930s it amazes the first travelers with whom he discusses his island theology and outlines the bases of his poetic system, which begins with the image as the foundation of the world.

Among those travelers were Juan Ramón Jiménez —
"Lezama, my friend, you are so sharp, so enthusiastic, so vibrant, one can keep talking about poetry
with you forever"; María Zambrano, who was then
writing her *Cuba secreta,* a veritable decalogue of
Orígenes; Doctor Pittaluga, of whom Lezama utters
what the condescending succession of travelers invited by the revolution will later coin as the image of
Lezama himself — "He was a gentleman and he was
learned. . . . He was a style personified, he knew how
to quote a classic or smoke a cigar with incompara-
ble form"; Luis Cernuda, Wallace Stevens, Karl
Vossler. . . .

As if his supreme agility and the brilliance of his
associations corresponded, through a law of opposites, to physical fixedness and a confinement both
domestic and Cuban, Lezama's culture encom-
passed, with the lion's glance that is one of the
Buddha's attributes at birth, *everything, at the same
time.* One simple page can string together, as in a
semantic mirage, an improvised, asymmetrical Pythagoreanism; Le Corbusier; a German chest covered with baroque reliefs; one of Brueghel's paintings; a majolica wall tile with an Algerian alms box

attached; a tambourine; the rococo Louis XV; Quentin La Tour; the Council of Trent; a scarlet quiver; El Greco; Swedenborg; Boehme; Baudry, who painted biscuit porcelain — to note only explicit references, since the scope of his connotations and bifurcations would encompass an encyclopedic totality.

Whenever I found myself in a place described by Lezama, I always *recognized it from his description* — so precise is what could very well be called his *clairvoyance:* a Tibetan monastery in the Himalayas; the faded green expanse of the Ceylonese rice fields; a head of Saint Anthony from the Museum of the Hot Springs; or the rose window of Notre Dame adjacent to the horizon line of the river. An entire metaphysics of the *right view* — one of Buddhism's guiding principles, according to the first sermon at Sarnath, in which Sakyamuni pointed the way to gazelles and disciples — could be derived from Lezama's visual acuteness, from the way he would spread out and focus his sight before fixing his gaze, as if only the absence and distance of the real object — whose mental image we contemplate — allowed it to create the impression of reality in the text. An entire science of signs: annihilate, obliterate, scratch out the referent in the distance so that, in the purity and nakedness of the signified, we are granted access to the majesty of the signifier, the concision of the letter. This explains, perhaps, the rigor in Lezama's "fixedness," the almost moral persistence of his immobility, as if things would vanish once they were perceived as literal, as if the rose window of Notre Dame, seen up close, would reduce the incandescence of its ciphers, the ardent ratio of its numbers to "an improvised, asymmetrical Pythagoreanism," as if beyond the *cosa mentale* all things underwent degradation and all that remained of being, which is external to the image, were simulacra or waste products of being.[7]

Lezama liked to quote this sentence of Pascal: "It's good to see and not to see, this is precisely the state of nature."

Poetry is *knowledge power.*

—

"A nice andantino pace." The appearance of this Italian diminutive constitutes an epiphany of the Cuban language. None of the versions of Spanish that have arisen in the Americas have been more devoted to the minuscule, the diminutive, as if twisted or miniaturized words lent themselves immediately to a complete survey of listening: the sonorous surroundings of a Japanese garden. Affection — the most Cuban emotion — borders on the drive to make smaller; reduction amuses and fascinates, brings closer. Cubans have always had an innate aversion to the monumental, which is manifested at the first opportunity by their *choteo,* that useless practical joke or mockery, that irruption of the parodic and slightly grotesque. How many sentences filled with stale oratory or foggy, vulgar lyricism have been ridiculed by a *trompetilla,* the Cuban version of a Bronx cheer, as if they were confronted with their sinister doubles, with their pretentiously paint-smeared impostures.

Juan Goytisolo used to point out how, contrary to all other countries throughout history, which have considered their wars — no matter what the damage actually amounted to — as incommensurate catastrophes or apocalyptic prefigurations, Cuba christened one of its wars the "little war." He also stressed the graphic, cartoonish impact of the phrase used to sanction every ruined fortune, shattered reputation, or public derision of a former hero: "His little altar collapsed!"

Listening to these oscillations, one could also read Lezama's page as a score of sudden tiny chords, the twists and reductions caused by the diminutive endings that enamel Cuban language with their fiesta of miniatures, like oiled baroque mechanisms always ready to unfurl their parade of sarcastic dwarves, lifting their feet, jangling their little coin-covered jackets.

—

"As clouds galloping, but then the ray of grace begins its work." Baroque stage settings, the Council of Trent's resplendent pedagogy, which resorted unreservedly to the most efficacious, the most explicitly theatrical means to dazzle the faithful, to gather them in the luminous cone filtered by a Borrominesque skylight; beneath the swirling angels of a ceiling by Pozzo, in a single, ascending, spiral movement. All this to achieve the greatest realism, the greatest palpability: mystery incarnate. All this to convince.

—

"You, no doubt, will understand my moods quite well." If only my life, although without the telos that inspired his, could configure sufficient symmetries, parallelisms, coincidences and complicities with Lezama's life to justify this empathy.

—

"Back to our dear bits of flesh." Assuming I have deciphered correctly "the actual design drawn by his pen — curly and capricious like the trimming that edges the carnation, his favorite flower   the lines of a handwriting that seemed to need no exclamation or question mark in order to leave signs of an incontestable opening, of a different vehemence."[8] I don't recognize this expression as an idiomatic Cuban phrase or remember having heard it in my childhood. It has the realistic ring, however, of an idiolect. Although we may be dealing with nothing more than a question of precedence, an idiomatic phrase, the anonymous knowledge common to everyone, is only the repetition, the image — coined, minted, and worn out by use — of something that thanks to a slight alteration of standard language was once a poet's discovery. And vice versa.

—

"Any interval would open a lacuna in the center of the work." A curious premonition, in temporal terms, of what in *Oppiano Licario* will be the formal structure. The whole story revolves around a lacuna, a textual absence, or *Súmula:* a Pythagorean key and gnostic summa of the world, to which we never gain access, and which a cyclone and a dog, equally infernal and inopportune, scatter irretrievably. A blank page, the illegible and lacunal mark of the loss that brings to a halt — or centers — the unfinished sequel to *Paradiso.*[9]

—

"Occasion an Easter or a christening." In addition to the comments above about Lezama's fidelity to the observation of Christian rituals, his sense of celebration at once Catholic and Cuban, it is necessary to remember that José Cemí's fate as a poet is identified with that of Christ as a son. This can be read in the first lines of *Paradiso.* Cemí loses his ability to breathe in front of the family servants, metaphors of the Trinity, and the book proceeds from that arrhythmia to a total recovery of breath: the Hesychastic rhythm of the poetry; he defines his life, beginning with the Mother's devotion, as an incarnation or mystery, and is finally recognized by Oppiano Licario thanks to his initials: J.C.[10]

—

"What makes the world revolve is nothing but universal misunderstanding; through misunderstanding the whole world reaches agreement. Because, unfortunately, if everyone were to understand each other, no one would ever get along." I have not found the exact quote in the same edition of Baudelaire's complete works I sent Lezama. But that paradox gives rise to a reading reactivated in the light of current psychoanalysis. The work's permanence, like the prism Lezama turns in order to assemble a phrase, is nothing more than the possibility, forever renewable, of yet another refraction by the sharp edge. Through the translucent other side, the ray of writing, apparently colorless and unified, will open into the rainbow's spreading beam.

Structured, informative language, with its knots and links, precedes us as a large, falsely efficient Other, as the fragile support of our understanding and communication. If we were to rely on this utilitarian simulacrum, on its fallacious guarantee, we would never understand each other. Only the faults, defects, omissions, lapses in that code permit the suggestion of the subject, permit a glimpse of true communication to outcrop on the compact, marblelike surface of language. Thus the distracted, absentminded listening of the analyst, who pays no attention to the inopportune jumble of composed discourse, to what the analysand thinks he is saying, but hears, rather, a second discourse, on the threshold of the perceptible, when the first discourse keels, reverses, breaks, vacillates, falls.

"Deep down, Chomsky's ideal speaker-listener is what Lacan refers to elsewhere as the subject-supposed-to-know, the subject supposed to know language completely, the subject supposed to know always what he says, and this unique, unchanging, impeccable individual, about whom one dreams, does not exist. Something would be gained, then, if the scientific consideration of this simple formulation of Lacan, which is a kind of fundamental truth, were to serve as a point of departure. Although this cannot be said quickly, it is a fundamental truth — because *misunderstanding is the essence of communication. The error of a considerable number of sciences that are legitimate sciences, however, is to imagine that a thorough understanding of things forms the essence of communication.*"[11]

—

"A plain of snow." Among the constants of Cuban poetry, patiently catalogued by Cintio Vitier, one finds a predictable paradox of cold, frost, snow; that is, a constellation of courage and sense metaphorized in a "noncoincidence with reality — a lack of fate, an inadequacy for profound human communion, an atmosphere of resentment and bitterness, a hidden life, desertion, desolation."[12]

—

"Saint Augustine called early for the existence of heretics." An attitude very Catholic in the splendor of its paradox: sin shapes part of the divine design, which, according to medieval *doxes,* needs shadows to highlight its forms and reliefs. Quoted by Claudel, Saint Augustine utters the *etiam peccata:* even sin serves the glory of God and the redemption of the world. Quoted by Lezama, he seems even more concerned with evil, a possible reminiscence of the heresy that gave rise to his teaching: a Manichaean dualism which makes Evil as active a principle as Good, and sees the struggle between these antagonists in the smallest image of divine manifestation. Like Saint Augustine, who prophesies that Antiquity will end with the taking of Rome, who finds himself alive during the twilight of knowledge, and who even wavers in the face of paganism, Lezama continually alludes to the undertow of barbarism in the disquiet of his final years, as he sees the Catholic society in which he has lived suddenly annihilated: for although he wrote on its margins, *against the current,* that society sustained his language and his faith.

The heresy Saint Augustine requires and rejects is Pelagianism. An ascetic born in Great Britain, Pelagius settled in Rome and attempted a dialogue with Augustine when he passed through Africa in 411. Like many Italian refugees, he continued on to Palestine.

Transforming Christianity into pure morality, the Pelagians maintained that man's essential task was to seek virtue, and that he could attain it — since evil in itself does not exist — thanks to his own free will. They went so far as to concede such minimal importance to original sin that they postulated the futility of baptism. Saint Augustine asserted the contrary, that man cannot save himself without God's intervention, without grace. Perhaps this explains why, centuries later, the members of Port Royal invoked him against the Jesuits. The disciples there did not believe, as did the Manichaeans, in an absolute evil that man should battle with complete devotion. But they did not differ radically from the Manichaeans, maintaining that evil was so strong, man could free himself from it only through grace.

One could weave a probable history of the West starting from this controversy. Until that time, Christianity, like the thought of Antiquity, sustained itself with externals, laws, principles, and obedience. From the moment grace intervenes, one poses questions about the ultimate source of all possible action: the I, the subject, or the external force of grace. Here begins the vast, torturous history of interiority.

One line of thought in the Middle Ages, and in Descartes, then, derived from Saint Augustine. Saint Thomas, on the other hand, subscribed to a return and recovery of Antiquity, whence, explicitly, arose the *Ulysses* and *Paradiso*.[13]

—

"This world creates harmony from disharmony." This famous phrase from Gracián's *El criticón* [The carper] closes the triad that Lezama sketches, for which he provides the background by joining the most distant and apparently dissimilar things in the ray of oblique knowledge. *Trivium* of alienation: around Lezama, from the time of his letter and even until his death, everything will seem like simulation and soft laughter, a discreet, general farce. Thanks to the collective consensus of appearance, to the misunderstanding and disorder promulgated in an almost carnivalesque manner, as well as to the category of truth, to inflated, vacuous discourse accepted as a norm and a moral code, the society of the simulacrum functions, survives, even prospers, as if in that fall man were contemplating an indolent telos-free image of his history, a manifestation — grotesque but as valid as any other — of his *potential*.

—

"That's why Baudelaire had to seek help from the devil of lucidity, a kind of [embodiment?] of alienation." I cannot quite decipher the word that follows *kind of;* it might be "embodiment," but the first stroke and the one after the letter *d* are debatable. I prefer, in any case, that this reading of Lezama end by calling, from the place of absence, as in *Oppiano Licario,* upon the reader's concurrence and complicity. The text thrives beyond death, although this may be in the uncertainty of the letter, in the theorem of its shadow. "I have only a few years left now before I experience the terrible crash of the beyond. But I have survived everything, and I will also survive death. Heidegger maintains that man is a being made for death; all poets, however, create resurrection, intone a triumphant hurrah in the face of death. If anyone thinks I exaggerate, he will end up trapped by disaster, the devil, and the circles of hell."[14]

NOTES TO THE NOTES

1. *Paradiso* (Mexico: Era, 1968), 17. (*Paradiso*, trans. Gregory Rabassa [Austin: University of Texas Press, 1974], 15. [Translation somewhat modified here. (Trans. note.)]

2. Referred to in "Página sobre Lezama" [Page about Lezama], which, along with the manuscript of a letter to his sister Eloísa, forms the back cover of his *Cartas (1939–1976)* [Letters] (Madrid: Orígenes, 1979). The letter I discuss here is not included in that volume and is unpublished.

3. Although the presence of the French classics, among them Racine himself, means that this period cannot be included among Lezama's *eras imaginarias* [imaginary eras] if we adhere to the strict definition of that term: ". . . the conviction that in imaginary eras, in historical periods, the image was expressed so frequently *that even though they did not provide great poets,* poetry was lived fully. No great poets appear between Virgil and Dante; nevertheless it is a time of great poetry. This is the period of the Merovingians when all of Europe fills with

exorcisms and wondrous occurrences. The common man is convinced that, like the men of the Old Testament, Charlemagne conquered Zaragoza when he was two hundred and twenty years old, and people set out on pilgrimages and constructed the great stone symbols." *La imagen como fundamento poético del mundo,* by Loló de la Torriente, in *Bohemia,* about 1960(?). Emphasis added.

4. *Lezama Lima, los grandes todos* (Montevideo: Arca, 1968), introduction and interviews by Armando Alvarez Bravo.

5. As evoked, and with the precision only possible for another member of *Orígenes,* by Lorenzo García Vega in *Los años de Orígenes* [The *Orígenes* years] (Caracas: Monte Avila, 1979).

6. In this same letter, Lezama evokes "an Easter or a christening," when he offers the metaphor of the happiness it would cause him to receive the complete works of Baudelaire.

7. The letter I discuss is dated 21 July 1969. A few days later, Lezama writes to his sister Eloísa, speaking this time about an invitation from UNESCO sent by César Fernández Moreno shortly after the one he

received from Seuil; he insists upon the impossibility of any trip and shortens drastically the possible stay he mentions to me. In my letter he says, "What I would like to do is spend a year in Paris or Madrid, resting and recuperating"; in Eloísa's letter he says, "I plan to spend a week in Paris and a month in Madrid."

"As I told you by phone, UNESCO has invited me to Paris to give a talk on Gandhi. I feel so despondent, so indolent and apathetic, that what at other times would have caused me great happiness is the cause of profound worries. To feel alone, without family, without support, can be so enervating that you lose your enthusiasm and decisiveness. María Luisa is encouraging me, and I think that, God willing, we'll make the trip; but these last ten years have been filled with such deep worries, that everything has become problematic and confused for us. If I do make the trip, I plan to spend a week in Paris and a month in Madrid."

To an inquiry about trips from the Centro de Investigaciones Literarias de la Habana [Center for Literary Research of Havana], Lezama answers: "There are some truly splendid trips, such as those a man can take from his bedroom to the bathroom along the corridors of his house, or parading through parks and bookstores. Why even consider the various means of transportation? I'm thinking about airplanes, where the travelers can walk only from nose to tail: this is not traveling. Travel is little more than a movement of the imagination. Travel is to recognize, recognize oneself, it is the loss of childhood and the admission of maturity. Goethe and Proust, those men of great diversity, almost never traveled. Their ship was the imago. I am the same: I have almost never left Havana. I acknowledge two reasons: each time I left, my bronchial tubes got worse; in addition, the memory of my father's death has floated at the center of every trip. Gide said that every voyage is a foretaste of death, an anticipation of the end. I don't travel: that's why I return to life." From "Interrogando a Lezama Lima" in *Recopilación de textos sobre José Lezama Lima* (Havana: Casa de las Américas, 1970).

8. Fina García Marruz, "Estación de gloria," in *Recopilación de textos sobre José Lezama Lima,* 270.

9. "In this way, the book that establishes a cosmic relation between the exceptions of nature and those

of form — the *Súmula* from which, after he snatches it from the dog, Cemí saves only one poem, configured for us as a blank page, although Lezama may have planned to add it when he finished the novel — is forever erased; equally unfinished is the book that, with *Paradiso,* will bring to a close the effort to found the island on the image, on the generative word. It drifts in the river, a mirror on the water, an endless flow, a scattering of ashes: the erased body of the founders." — Severo Sarduy, "*Oppiano Licario:* the book that could not end," *Vuelta* 18 (May 1978), 32. Also *Point of Contact* (Winter 1981), 123.

10. Julio Ortega, "Aproximaciones a *Paradiso,*" *Imagen* 40, supplement (1–15 Jan. 1969), 9–16. Reprinted in *Recopilación de textos sobre José Lezama Lima.*

11. Jacques-Alain Miller, *Cinco conferencias caraqueñas sobre Lacan* (Caracas: Editorial Ateneo de Caracas, 1980), 42. Emphasis added.

12. Cintio Vitier, *Lo cubano en la poesía* (Universidad Central de las Villas, 1958), 486.

13. Henri Marrou, "Le pélagianisme," Jean Da-

nielou and Henri Marrou, *Nouvelle histoire de l'eglise*, I, *Des origines à Grégoire le Grand* (Paris: Seuil, 1963), 450–59.

14. *Recopilación de textos sobre José Lezama Lima.*

Translators' Afterword

Severo Sarduy's concise, eloquent preface to *Christ on the Rue Jacob* provides the reader with sufficient orientation to his understanding of "epiphany" and "autobiography." His preface is almost an epitaph, like the mock-epitaph he writes for the brash Dolores Rondón, a character in his novel *From Cuba with a Song,* as she marches through each stage of her predestined life toward death. His preface subtly illuminates that the pieces in *Christ on the Rue Jacob* (and, one might add, his two other final books) are a kind of will and testament he leaves to his readers. It remains for the translators, however, to add a few words about Sarduy himself and about their own work with *El Cristo de la Rue Jacob.*

Sarduy was born in 1937 in Camagüey, Cuba, and he died in 1993 in Paris, where he had lived since 1960. He was both a painter and a versatile and prolific writer. As an avant-garde novelist he published *Gestos* (Gestures, 1963), *De donde son los cantantes* (*From Cuba with a Song*, 1967), *Cobra* (1972), *Maitreya* (1978), *Colibrí* (Hummingbird, 1983), and *Cocuyo* (Firefly, 1990). He was also a poet known for such works as *Un testigo perenne y delatado* (A witness perennial and betrayed, 1985) and *Un testigo fugaz y disfrazado* (A witness fleeting and disguised, 1993); a playwright, who published *Para la voz* (*For Voice*, 1978); and an essayist, whose best-known books are *Escrito sobre un cuerpo* (*Written on a Body*, 1969), *Barroco* (Baroque, 1974) and *La simulación* (Simulation, 1982).

His last two books were both published posthumously: *Epitafios* (Epitaphs), a volume of poetry and aphorisms that he titled in homage to his imminent death from AIDS; and *Pájaros de la playa* (Beach birds), a novel in which he simultaneously returned to the principal figures of his previous fiction and probed the future by recording the experience of dying from what he named *el Mal* (the Malady). A stark and restrained work, *Pájaros de la playa* is a sobering novel to read; it also offers a decided serenity, yet it by no means lacks the playfulness and self-consciousness that Sarduy required of his writing and of his own life.

Although "postmodern" was not a term on everybody's lips when his first novels appeared in the 1960s, one could say that the disjunctures and often disconcerting mix of the sacred and satirical in Sarduy's work are exemplary of postmodernism. As a textural writer and a textual painter, as a reveler in literal and figurative transvestism, he transgressed genres and genders, cultural and linguistic borders. An exiled Cuban devoted to Baroque poetics, *santería*, Maoism, Tibetan Buddhism, and French theory (among his close friends were Roland Barthes and Jacques Lacan), he deconstructed logocentrism in witty, lyrical, densely rigorous narratives that trace the fragmented subject's relentless self-quest as well as the arabesques of today's cultural and political realities. Despite the playful, subversive irreverence in his life and writing, Sarduy had a profound commitment to Eastern — indeed, to many — forms of spirituality. This means that he is a difficult writer to read and one impossible to classify, but in fact he characterizes the "place" of Latin America in

Western civilization perhaps more authentically than some of his more accessible "mainstream" colleagues.

Our decision to translate *Christ on the Rue Jacob* can be explained simply. Several years ago, after we had each published translations of Sarduy's work, we met and began to correspond. As we spoke of Sarduy, we each became aware of instances in which the other's translations had coincided with or differed from her own, with respect to some of the most challenging aspects of his style. We wondered if a translation we prepared together would bear distinct individual characteristics, and we agreed to undertake a joint project. *Christ on the Rue Jacob* appealed to us both; the short pieces included in it not only spanned all of Sarduy's writing, but also dealt specifically — albeit at times metaphorically — with his aesthetics, and would therefore require us to address directly questions and principles of translation. In addition, the format of the book was conducive to our collaborative work, which by necessity would be carried out at a distance. We divided the sections as follows: with the exception of Sarduy's preface and "Letter from

Lezama," which we shared, Jill prepared preliminary versions of "Because It's Real" and "On an Autumn Night, I Think of My Friends," and Carol prepared preliminary versions of "Archaeology of the Skin," "Unity of Place," and "Unity of Figure." Those versions were exchanged and revisions made jointly. Although each made the final decisions for the sections she had translated initially, many of those decisions occurred only after considerable discussion, and we share responsibility for them all.

To work collaboratively on a translation of *Christ on the Rue Jacob* was to participate in a complex reenactment of the single, slow, meticulous gesture of repetition that appears in so many of the pieces in this book. It was to consider, in a way quite different from the considerations in which one engages when working alone, the exact nature of Sarduy's "meticulousness" or precision in relation to his obsessive repetitions — always highly allusive and rarely identical. Such repetitions never fail to challenge the conventional definition of "accurate," and that challenge becomes more far intense when one is presented with two versions, both of which could be considered accurate. Sarduy (and the Spanish lan-

guage, one might add with a Borgesian nod) turns
rhetoric into poetry. In our differing versions we jug-
gled between lyrical and literal, and chose what we
heard as the particular stress and needs of each
instance, as in "fijeza," which Jill has elsewhere
translated as "stillness" and Carol as "fixity."
"Fijeza" may sound more like "stillness" in tone but
means more precisely "fixed in time and space." We
used "fixedness" on this occasion — favoring accuracy — because Sarduy was referring explicitly to the
title of a book by Lezama Lima. Not wishing to
impose theoretical or academic jargon, on other
occasions we opted for a less rigid definition of
accuracy, particularly when translating Sarduy's
often ironic use of philosophical and psychoanalytic
terms. Following Sarduy's lead, we also employed
brief notes when we believed they were necessary.
What consistently proved at once frustrating and
helpful to us were Sarduy's own rather paradoxical
assertions about the relative unimportance of the
stylistic features or "techniques" that characterize
this work, and, simultaneously, about the exactness
of the ritualistic detail that is absolutely necessary if
the reader is to be placed, as Sarduy himself had
been, "in touch with something."

Since Sarduy died as we were beginning to work intensively on *Christ on the Rue Jacob,* to translate this book collaboratively was also to have companionship. Death pervades the volume, and had we not been able to comment between us about Sarduy's passing, we might not have been able to appreciate adequately the extent to which the approach to death Sarduy's epiphanies suggest is also an approach to life. Deliberately impious and sentimental, but neither iconoclastic nor maudlin, the pieces manifest an often disconcerting heterogeneity, in which conventional dichotomies are jumbled in startling, unexpected ways. To read them carefully is to rethink one's sense of epiphany itself, to recognize that the "sacred" and the "sordid" can exist concurrently, that, at the same time and with the same gesture, it is possible to render homage and to ridicule mercilessly. In short, the brief parabolic incidents in *Christ on the Rue Jacob* demonstrate, well before it becomes explicit in *Pájaros de la playa,* the drive that informed Sarduy's last works. This drive could be expressed as an infinitive phrase or a "pure" action in which the Western definition of the self — and, implicitly, of all exclusive boundaries — is questioned: Train yourself not to be.

How might such a directive affect the translation of Sarduy's writing? Surprisingly, perhaps, an answer can be offered rather simply. With respect to one's general approach or "theory," a response has already been anticipated in our comments about accuracy and the search for balance between "detail" and "style." With respect to practice — and, not coincidentally, as an indication that Sarduy's infinitive phrase respects no distinction between practice and theory — a single example, that of the quotation in "Tangier" from *Naked Lunch,* should suffice.

When one searches through Burroughs's novel for the passage Sarduy cites, so as to insert the "original" English into the translation, it becomes evident that, although the bulk of the paragraph does indeed correspond to an identifiable passage, some of the sentences have been taken from other sections of the book, and there is one sentence that Sarduy has apparently added himself. There are also snippets from *Naked Lunch* woven into Sarduy's own words. This appropriation affirms Sarduy's evocation, at the beginning of "Tangier," of Roland Barthes's comment about the Socco Chico as "the site of writing," and it reminds the informed reader that Barthes's comments occur in *The Pleasure of the Text* and that Barthes made his remark in reference to Sarduy's novel *Cobra*. Neither of these books is named in "Tangier," but they each make an appearance there, evoked in Sarduy's prose just as his description of Tangier had once been evoked in the prose of Barthes. Thus the snippets of *Naked Lunch* also serve to illustrate Sarduy's sense of "ownership" and to offer a translator an instructive example of the admiring yet appropriative and allusive way in which he works with his sources.

"Source" to Sarduy — reading here in an unorthodox fashion rather than adhering strictly to the rules of etymology — suggests both "ore" and "sore." "Sour," it is also "our," and at bottom, when reduced to the smallest "unit of meaning," it yields "or" — not an absolute but an alternative way of perceiving, another text. As translators, in order to place the English-language reader "in touch" with that "or" or that "something," we endeavored to bear in mind meticulously the exactness of the incidents in *Christ on the Rue Jacob*. We also endeavored, however, to adopt Sarduy's own effort "not to be" — to conceive of our work within the repetition illustrated by the motions of the street cleaner of Mexico City or of Sarduy himself as he painted or wrote. The same dog with a different collar, with emphasis on both "same" and "different."

We would like, in closing, to thank those friends and fellow scholars, among them Octavio Armand, Eduardo González, Enrico Mario Santí, Alejandro Varderi, and Eliot Weinberger, who have helped clarify meanings and allusions. In the absence of Severo, whom we consulted in the past, we are grateful for their supportive presence.

— Suzanne Jill Levine and Carol Maier

SUZANNE JILL LEVINE's translations include works by Guillermo Cabrera Infante, Julio Cortázar, José Donoso, Manuel Puig, and Adolfo Bioy Casares.

CAROL MAIER has translated Rosa Chacel, Octavio Armand, Carlota Caulfield, and Carmen Martín Gaite.